"I heard you say you was goin' after el Espectro.

If'n you'll take my advice, Clint, you'll forget all about tanglin' with that Mex devil."

"I'm not exactly looking forward to it, Joe," Clint admitted.

"You wanna know about el Espectro? I can tell you where to find out all about him."

The Gunsmith turned to gaze at the aged hostler.

"You can read about the dead man who rides a white stallion in the Book of Revelation," Joe replied. *"I looked, and behold a pale horse: and his name that sat on him was Death . . ."*

Don't miss any of the lusty, hard-riding action in the new Charter Western series, THE GUNSMITH:

THE GUNSMITH #1: MACKLIN'S WOMEN
THE GUNSMITH #2: THE CHINESE GUNMEN
THE GUNSMITH #3: THE WOMAN HUNT
THE GUNSMITH #4: THE GUNS OF ABILENE
THE GUNSMITH #5: THREE GUNS FOR GLORY
THE GUNSMITH #6: LEADTOWN
THE GUNSMITH #7: THE LONGHORN WAR
THE GUNSMITH #8: QUANAH'S REVENGE
THE GUNSMITH #9: HEAVYWEIGHT GUN
THE GUNSMITH #10: NEW ORLEANS FIRE
THE GUNSMITH #11: ONE-HANDED GUN
THE GUNSMITH #12: THE CANADIAN PAYROLL
THE GUNSMITH #13: DRAW TO AN INSIDE DEATH
THE GUNSMITH #14: DEAD MAN'S HAND
THE GUNSMITH #15: BANDIT GOLD
THE GUNSMITH #16: BUCKSKINS AND SIX-GUNS
THE GUNSMITH #17: SILVER WAR
THE GUNSMITH #18: HIGH NOON AT LANCASTER

And coming next month:

THE GUNSMITH #20: THE DODGE CITY GANG

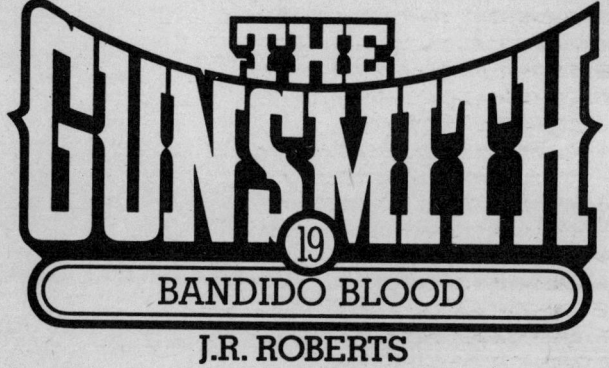

J.R. ROBERTS

CHARTER BOOKS, NEW YORK

To Linda Smith-Hancharick

THE GUNSMITH #19:
BANDIDO BLOOD

A Charter Book / published by arrangement with
the author

PRINTING HISTORY
Charter Original / August 1983

All rights reserved.
Copyright © 1983 by Robert J. Randisi
This book may not be reproduced in whole
or in part, by mimeograph or any other means,
without permission. For information address:
The Berkley Publishing Group, 200 Madison Avenue,
New York, N.Y. 10016

ISBN: 0-441-30890-2

Charter Books are published by The Berkley Publishing Group,
200 Madison Avenue, New York, N.Y. 10016.
PRINTED IN THE UNITED STATES OF AMERICA

ONE

"How the hell did Joe let this happen to you?" Clint Adams muttered as he unscrewed a bolt from the frame of a .44-caliber Winchester carbine.

Joe Saunders owned a livery stable in Brookstown, Texas. When Clint arrived in the small border town with his wagon and his prized Arabian gelding Duke, Joe had been delighted at the chance to earn a handsome profit for taking care of the rig and horses. When Clint told him he'd pay extra to be certain everything—especially Duke—received special treatment, Joe guessed his customer's identity.

"By golly!" the hostler exclaimed. "You're the Gunsmith, ain't you? I heard tell you always pay special for this big black beauty of a hoss. Yes sir, Duke here is almost as famous as you are! Can see why too, 'cause he's purely the most beautiful hoss I ever did lay eyes on! Hey, you are the Gunsmith, ain't you?"

With a weary sigh, Clint Adams admitted that some folks—too many folks in his opinion—called him the Gunsmith. He also mentally cursed the newspaperman who had given him that monicker years ago. The journalist had discovered that Clint, who was then a deputy sheriff in Oklahoma, repaired and modified firearms as a hobby. The newspaperman had already been working on a story about Deputy Adams, so he decided to tack on the Gunsmith title for a little extra color.

It proved to be the beginning of a legend. Clint Adams had suddenly received unwanted fame as a lightning-fast draw, unbeatable with a gun. The fact that Clint decided to give up wearing a badge and became a genuine gunsmith, or that his skill with his modified double-action .45 Colt more than equaled the legend, didn't make Clint any happier with the title or the reputation that went with it.

At least, however, Joe Saunders was aware that Clint was a real gunsmith and not just a gunfighter with a fancy nickname. He'd heard that Clint Adams traveled throughout the West in his wagon, picking up work. It just happened Joe had an old Winchester that sorely needed repairs and he'd be mighty honored if the Gunsmith would personally fix it.

So Clint and Joe made a deal which pleased both men. The Gunsmith would repair the Winchester as payment for Joe's services as a hostler. Joe would be able to tell about his encounter with the celebrity to anyone who cared to listen, displaying his carbine as he spun his tale. For Clint's part, he usually paid about five dollars to see to his wagon and horses, while he seldom charged more than a dollar or two for simple gunsmithing on a single weapon.

But then he saw Joe Saunders's Winchester. The gun looked as if it had been used as a garden tool. The barrel was rusty and pitted, the magazine had been dented and the mainspring to the trigger was broken. Simple repairs, shit!

Clint had to disassemble the carbine, run a rod with a wire-bore brush through the barrel and scrub half a pint of solvent along the muzzle before it was clean. Most of the rust had to be filed down and oiled, but the weapon needed a fresh blueing job to look halfway decent again. Clint decided to skip any efforts to restore the Winchester's former beauty and concentrated on making the weapon serviceable and safe to shoot—although he doubted that Joe would fire it much anyway. The tubular magazine was too badly dented to repair so it had to be replaced. The same proved true for the trigger spring, the hammer and the firing pin. Parts alone would have come to at least six dollars and the labor would have cost at least four under ordinary circumstances. Some deal!

"Joe must have just let you sit around and get rusty after he broke your parts," Clint said. As was his habit when he was alone—and he was alone most of the time—he spoke to the gun as he worked.

"I'd like to get you all fixed up before five o'clock," he continued, attaching the new tubular magazine under the barrel. "I met a pretty lady who works at the local haberdashery. Bought a new hat I really don't need and can hardly afford, but it gave me a chance to talk to her. She's Annie Michaels and she's about twenty-three years old and she doesn't have a husband or a beau. I'm going to meet her when she gets off work and take her to dinner and—if I've read the twinkle in her eye correctly—we might just wind up back here in this very room. . . ."

Knuckles rapping on the door interrupted his conversation with the Winchester. Clint told the visitor to come in as he placed the screwdriver on the table where he worked and dropped his hand to the butt of his .45 Colt on his right hip. The Gunsmith had enemies he didn't even know about. There'd always be young gunhawks looking for a reputation and people out to avenge a friend or relative Clint had put in Boot Hill, not to mention the fellows he'd sent to prison who may have been released or even escaped and happened to be in Brookstown. He couldn't afford to be careless or allow himself to be caught off guard. Not if he planned to stay alive.

The door opened slowly and the visitor peered into the room. Annie Michaels looked at Clint and then glanced about to see if anyone else was present. Clint realized she'd heard him talking to himself (which sounded less loco than talking to a Winchester carbine), and she naturally thought he might not be alone. Clint hoped Annie had only been able to hear his voice and not the exact words he'd used in contemplating his evening.

Annie was an attractive girl with bright red hair worn in a ponytail, which made her round, soft face seem very young. In a few years, the girl might become fat, but her current plumpness only accented her breasts and buttocks. Her wide blue eyes and bowlike mouth were her most appealing features.

"Hello, Annie," the Gunsmith said, rising from his chair. He glanced at the turnip-shaped watch he'd placed on the table beside the Winchester. "It's only four o'clock. . . ."

"I know," she replied, stepping inside and closing the door. Annie inspected the Gunsmith with frank interest. "I'm early."

"Did something come up?" Clint asked. "I hope you didn't decide to cancel our date."

"No," the girl assured him. "Are you working on that gun?" She pointed at the carbine.

"Yeah." He rolled his eyes with frustration. "I've

been working on it for over two hours. I haven't had to do so much rebuilding, replacing and modifications on a gun since I converted my Colt to fire double action."

"Double action?" Annie raised a delicate eyebrow.

"Most guns have to be cocked each time before you fire a round," Clint explained as he picked up the screwdriver. "That's single action. A double-action firearm self-cocks when you squeeze the trigger."

"And because it doesn't have to be cocked each time you can fire it faster, right?" Annie observed.

"Exactly." Clint smiled, pleased that the girl was paying attention and *thinking* about the subject—which was one of his favorites to discuss. "Shooting double action is faster, but it reduces accuracy. That's why, when I have time, I usually cock the hammer and fire single action."

"Do you have to shoot a gun in a hurry very often?" she asked.

"It has happened from time to time," Clint confessed. "All I have to do with this carbine is put the bolts back into the gun and secure the magazine. That'll only take a minute. Then we can see about dinner."

"Are you hungry right yet, Clint?" the girl inquired.

"Well," he began as he tightened the bolts into the frame of the Winchester, "I can wait awhile, sure. Is there something else you'd rather do first?"

"It's pretty rare to meet an attractive, interesting man in a town like Brookstown," Annie went on. "When we met, you felt the same way I did, right?"

"I hope so." Clint smiled, hoping he hadn't misread the suggestive glitter in her eyes when they'd first met nor misunderstood her words now.

"Then we both figured we'd wind up in this room," Annie said candidly. "In that bed."

"Yes," the Gunsmith admitted. "I want to make love to you, but that's not all I had in mind when I asked you to have dinner with me. I'd like to talk to you and listen to what you have to say."

The redhead laughed. "You don't have to be romantic or pretend you won't ride out of town when you've finished with the business that brought you here."

"I told you when we met that I'd only be in Brookstown for a couple days. And I *will* ride out of here then, just like I said. As for being romantic—what's wrong with that?"

"You just don't have to be if it's for my benefit."

"Let's just say it serves us both. I need to treat a lady like a lady. When a man spends most of his time alone on the trail, he misses the sound of a woman's voice. He wants to look at her and smell her perfume and hold her hand. He wants to enjoy that special kind of gentle companionship only a woman can provide."

"That's nice, Clint." Annie smiled as she drew closer and slipped her arms around his neck. "But right now I've got something else on my mind."

"Maybe after we've taken care of that," he replied, his arms encircling her waist, "you'll develop an appetite for dinner."

"One appetite at a time," she said before their lips met.

TWO

The kiss started sweet and tender, but their mutual passion soon added fire to their touch. Despite Clint's apparent calm, he'd felt the blaze of desire stir in his loins the moment Annie Michaels had entered the room. He slid his tongue along the edges of her teeth, then slowly used it to caress the sides and roof of her mouth.

Annie shivered in response to his skillful kiss and her tongue probed his mouth in a similar manner. Their hands gradually explored each other's bodies. Annie's fingers unbuttoned Clint's shirt to stroke the hair on his chest while the Gunsmith's palm rubbed the small of her back. His hands roamed over her ribs and slowly made their way to her breasts.

His tender caresses had already excited the girl and increased her anticipation before she felt his fingers gently squeeze her left breast. Clint felt the nipple, erect beneath the fabric of her dress, and knew she was ready. Annie's groping hands confirmed this as she proved even more bold than Clint. The Gunsmith hummed with pleasure when her hands found his hardened manhood.

They helped each other shed their clothes in their haste to satisfy the mounting desire that burned in them both. Even as they moved to the bed, they were still unfastening buttons and buckles. When Annie finally stood naked before the Gunsmith he examined her with appreciation. The girl's unfettered breasts were large and heavy, their magnificent pink-tipped nipples firm and inviting. Her full breasts and hips suited her doll-like face and made her appealing and cuddly as well as pretty.

In contrast, the Gunsmith's physique was lean with well-toned muscles. Almost twice as old as the girl, Clint was still fit, although more than one scar revealed he'd had experiences that were less than gentle. Annie combed her fingers through the carpet of hair on his chest, slowly moving her hand to his flat abdomen and finally to his unrestricted penis.

She stroked his member until it swelled to full length. Then Annie lowered herself to one knee and gazed at Clint's genitals as if inspecting a diamond necklace. The Gunsmith wondered if her boldness were artificial. He'd had few virgins and generally avoided them because they tend to expect too much in a relationship which, in Clint's case, couldn't include commitments of any kind.

His apprehension proved to be needless as Annie cupped his balls in her palm and took him in her mouth. The girl's lips slipped over the head of his maleness and slowly traveled up the fleshy shaft to the root. Her head began to move back and forth, her mouth riding his throbbing cock with eagerness and ability that revealed she was not a novice in the arts of lovemaking.

Clint felt himself near the brink as Annie's mouth moved faster. He was about to warn her when she stopped and quickly moved to the bed and lay down on her back, her legs parted in invitation. The Gunsmith joined her on the mattress, his hands stroking her flesh as his lips, tongue and teeth tenderly stimulated her breasts. The girl moaned with pleasure and pulled him closer. She obviously didn't want to wait any longer, so Clint mounted her.

Annie immediately found his erection and steered it to where it belonged. Both sighed with pleasure as he entered. Clint slowly gyrated his hips to work himself deeper. The girl squirmed beneath him, clinging to his shoulders and neck. She gasped as he began pumping his member inside her. Annie's nails bit into his flesh and she gasped to the rhythm of Clint's thrusting manhood.

The Gunsmith lunged again and again, increasing the tempo until the girl cried out in ecstatic delight. She was an energetic lover, but she hadn't drawn Clint's seed from him yet. Still joined together, they rested for a few minutes before he began grinding and thrusting again. They rode to glory together, breathing hard in passionate labor as they reached the summit. The girl convulsed in a wild orgasm while Clint's swollen member finally discharged its load.

"Oh, Clint," Annie purred as she snuggled close to him, still connected in the closest physical manner possible for a man and a woman. "That was wonderful."

"Yes," he whispered his agreement as he kissed her ear.

"Can we do it one more time before we have dinner?"

"I don't see why not—"

Their pillow talk was interrupted by the urgent rapping of knuckles on the door. The girl gasped and Clint instinctively reached for the headboard where he usually hung his gunbelt before climbing into bed. However, in his haste to make love to Annie, Clint hadn't placed the holstered revolver in its customary position. It was on the floor, buried under a bundle of their clothing.

"Mr. Adams?" a man's voice called through the door. "Mr. Adams, are you awake?"

"Oh, shit," Clint muttered under his breath.

"Maybe he ain't in his room," a man with an East Texas accent remarked from the opposite side of the door.

"The desk clerk assured us he was here," the first voice declared in a Texas drawl that revealed a formal education.

"He mighta slipped out when the clerk wasn't lookin'," the second man suggested. "If'n the door ain't locked, maybe we oughta just go inside and wait for him to come back."

The Gunsmith stifled a groan. Neither he nor Annie had locked the door.

"Don't let them in here!" Annie rasped into Clint's ear.

"You fellas hold on a minute!" the Gunsmith shouted at the door. "I—I don't want to be disturbed. I'm busy."

"We must talk to you, Mr. Adams," the cultured voice insisted.

"Wait for me down in the hotel lobby, damn it!" Clint snapped.

"Don't, Andy!" the East Texan warned.

Suddenly, the door burst open and a slender figure dressed in a tweed suit capped by a white stetson entered. The girl squealed in horror and grabbed the bed sheets to cover her nakedness. Clint withdrew from her, his penis now dangling limply, and lunged

BANDIDO BLOOD 11

from the bed. His visitor, however, held up his hands to reveal he held no weapon. The man's mouth formed a small oval as he stared dumbfounded at the Gunsmith and Annie Michaels.

"Uh," he began awkwardly, "I apologize for this . . . interruption, but I really must—"

"You really must get out of here before I get hold of my gun!" Clint snapped. He was angry and embarrassed as he stood stark naked over the pile of clothing which concealed his gunbelt.

"Jesus, Andy!" a paunchy bearded man in the hallway cried. "You're gonna get us killed!"

Andy, the man in the tweed suit, ignored his friend's plea. "I must talk with you, Mr. Adams. . . ."

"So talk to him!" Annie shouted as she wrapped a sheet togalike around herself and stomped from the bed. "I'm getting out of here before you all make such a ruckus the manager, the sheriff and maybe even Reverend James Michaels—who happens to be my uncle—all head over here to see what the hell is going on!"

"Annie . . ." Clint groped for words to calm her, but he realized that was impossible. He was still too pissed off himself. "You two fellas wait in the lobby!"

"Then you'll talk with us?" Andy asked eagerly.

"Yeah," the Gunsmith sighed. "There's nothing left to do but talk, is there?"

THREE

Clint tried to pacify Annie after their unexpected visitors left, but the girl was too furious to listen. She angrily pulled on her clothing and stormed out of the Gunsmith's room. Clint donned his clothes as well, went downstairs and found the two strangers who'd ruined his evening waiting for him in the lobby. The man in the city suit rose from his chair.

"I'm really terribly sorry about this, Mr. Adams," he began.

"Do us both a favor and don't mention it again," the Gunsmith warned. "Now, what do you two want?"

"Perhaps introductions are in order," the man in the suit suggested. "I'm Congressman Andrew Woodland and this is Fred Barsa." He gestured toward his stocky companion.

"That's wonderful, Congressman," Clint muttered.

"Well, you see, Fred owns a ranch a few miles west of Brookstown near the border," Woodland said. "I was a lawyer in Houston before I got into politics. I still have part ownership of the law firm and I've been thinking about buying a ranch."

"Hold on," Clint said, glaring at Woodland. "If the federal government is asking me for another favor, the answer is no. I didn't care for the deal Washington gave me the last time."

"Hell, this ain't no government business," Fred Barsa declared. "Andy here has a habit of talkin' too much and takin' too long to get to the heart of the matter. Guess that's why he went into politics. Natural talent for borin' folks with details. Need that for filibusters, I reckon."

"You running for office too, friend?" Clint asked dryly.

"All right," Woodland declared firmly. "My daughter has been kidnapped and I want you to get her back for me. Is that plain enough?"

The Gunsmith's eyebrows rose. "Maybe you'd better bore me with a few more details after all," he said, sinking into one of the chairs in the lobby.

"Very well." Woodland returned to his chair. "As I'm sure you noticed, Fred and I are old friends. Well, he's hit on some hard times and he can use some help with the mortgage. I'm interested in the cattle business, so I came down here to look over his ranch and to see if we could both profit by my becoming a silent partner in the business. Marsha, my daughter, hadn't been away from the capital for quite a while and she wanted a change of scene, so she came with me."

"Andy and Marsha come to my ranch the other day," Barsa added. "Yesterday morning, my foreman and me took Andy out for a look-see over the ranch to show him what all we got. When we come back, somebody had hit my house. The bastards killed my housekeeper, Lupe. Cut her up like a butchered steer and pinned a note to her chest with a knife."

"Of course, Marsha was gone," Woodland said,

extracting a wrinkled piece of paper from his pocket. "Here is the note, Mr. Adams. Please read it."

Clint took the paper. The handwriting on the letter was small and remarkably neat. Brown stains of dried blood on the paper were an ugly contrast to the author's penmanship, although it underscored the meaning of the words of the note.

Congressman Woodland:
  Your daughter will be staying with us for a few days. How long will depend on you. If you want her back, you will pay us five thousand dollars in American currency. Send someone to deliver the payment to the town of Grajo in Sonora. When he arrives, he need only mention that he wishes to contact el Espectro. Someone will relay the information to me and I will contact your man as quickly as possible.
  I trust I needn't remind you, Congressman, that Sonora is in Mexico and neither you nor your government has any authority in my country. Your lawmen and soldiers can not legally take any action against me south of the border. If you think the *federales* will help you, you are a fool. Even if they agreed to do so, they could never find me. They have been trying to hunt down el Espectro, but they've never succeeded. They no longer try for they know I am Death.
  It would be even more foolish to try to hire mercenaries to send into Mexico. They would be totally powerless against me. Besides, such nonsense would take time, Congressman, and you have little of that. Your daughter is a beautiful girl. She is young and fair with hair the color of the sun and eyes like the morning sky. Already my men lust for her. I can control my men, who also fear the power of el Espectro, yet, as the days pass, I will be less inclined to deny my followers what they desire. You do not want your lovely Marsha ravaged and mistreated. You do not want her to die by the knife as this servant woman has died. Contact me quickly, Congressman, or your daughter's blood will be on your hands.

The note was signed "el Espectro," the letters scrawled boldly across the bottom of the paper. Clint frowned and returned the note to Woodland. He felt as if he needed to wash his hands after holding the kidnapper's letter.

"Fred tells me this Espectro is a bandit leader in Mexico," the congressman said. "I know that's hard to believe because his letter is well written. . . ."

"If we were talking about any other *bandido* I'd be apt to dismiss this letter as a forgery and figure your daughter took off with a lover and left the note to try to trick you out of five thousand dollars," the Gunsmith remarked.

"Now, see here, Adams!" Woodland snapped. "Marsha would never do anything like—"

"Easy, friend." Clint held up a hand for silence. "I said if it was any other bandit except el Espectro."

"Heard about him, eh?" Barsa inquired.

The Gunsmith nodded. "El Espectro—the Ghost—has been operating south of the border for about five years now. Witnesses claim he looks like a dead man—thin, pale and cloaked in a black shroud. The *peónes* believe he's an evil spirit, a corpse that rides from the depths of Hell on a great white stallion."

"What do you make of that, Mr. Adams?" Woodland asked.

"I'd be apt to dismiss el Espectro as a ghost story—no pun intended—if he was supposed to be able to stare at a man and stop his heart or put a hex on a village, but they say he brings hellfire out of the barrel of a gun and that's the sort of witchcraft I can understand.

"A while back, I made a trip to Mexico to return a chest of gold stolen from their national treasury," Clint continued. "I spent some time with a *federale* general who asked me about el Espectro. The *bandido* is supposed to speak fluent English and the *federales* figure he might be a renegade *gringo*. Of course, his Spanish is just as good, but General Moreno had hoped I might be able to give him some information about any American outlaws that might fit el Espectro's description. The *federales* have no clue as to the guy's real identity. All they know is he commands one hell of a *bandido* gang—about fifty of the most vicious killers in Mexico. Moreno considers el Espectro to be the smartest, most dangerous bandit chief in the country and he admitted the *federales* have been unable to deal with the Ghost."

"Do you think there's any hope that I'll get my daughter back alive?" Woodland asked.

"Not if you pay the ransom," Clint answered. "El Espectro isn't going to let your daughter free after she's seen his headquarters. He can't afford to take the chance that she might remember enough to give the *federales* adequate information to lead them to his lair."

"Then he may have already . . ." Woodland swallowed hard. "Marsha might already be dead."

The Gunsmith was blunt. "That's true. She might be dead, but the Ghost might keep her alive for two reasons. First, he may figure he'll have to produce evidence to prove she's alive before you'll pay the ransom. Second . . . well, he might plan to use her to make an additional profit."

"You mean he'll ask for more money in the future?" the congressman asked.

"No," Clint replied. "I doubt that because he probably figures you'd be less apt to pay a second time and more likely to pressure the Mexican government into taking action. Juarez is probably the best leader in Mexican history and he's made a hard effort to maintain good relations with the United States. Pressure from Washington might eventually result in a massive *federale* manhunt for el Espectro. The Ghost could also fear you'd hire a couple dozen gunfighters and send them to handle the matter. Don't be fooled by el Espectro's boasts that he's invincible. Notice how eager he is for you to act quickly? He doesn't want this to take any longer than necessary in order to protect himself.''

"Then what other profit might he—" Fred Barsa began. "Oh, God! No! You're thinkin' of white slavery, ain't you?"

Clint sighed. "If Marsha is a beautiful blonde, as the Ghost describes her, she'll fetch a handsome price if he sells her to a brothel south of the border. If he has the right contacts, he could even transport her out of Mexico to Guatemala, Honduras or even Nicaragua or Colombia."

"Mr. Adams," Woodland began.

"Clint," the Gunsmith urged.

"Clint." The congressman smiled weakly. "I wanted to hire you to take the money to Sonora to try to make the exchange for Marsha's release."

"Me?" Clint raised his eyebrows. "Why me? I've been to Mexico a couple of times, but I don't know the country that well and I barely speak enough Spanish to get by down there."

"Oh, we got a feller to work as a guide and translator," Barsa declared. "Feller named Juan Lopez."

"But Juan doesn't have your reputation, Clint," Woodland added.

"As a fast gun?" Clint frowned.

"Your ability is legendary," the congressman admitted. "It's said you're the fastest, most accurate gunfighter in the West."

"I'm not a gunfighter."

"If the term offends you, I'm sorry," Woodland assured him. "But the fact remains you've killed a lot of men with that modified Colt forty-five."

"Including some pretty fearsome pistolmen," Barsa added. "Con Macklin, the Dragon Kid, Stansfield Lloyd, Dale Leighton . . ."

"But more important than your skill with a gun," Woodland went on, "you also have a reputation for honesty and integrity. You're a man of honor and principles. The type of man I can trust to take five thousand dollars to Mexico to make the trade for my daughter."

"If you pay el Espectro, whatever chance Marsha may have will be gone," the Gunsmith warned.

"What other choice do I have?" Woodland asked helplessly. "You tell me the *federales* haven't been able to deal with this bandit."

"But they didn't know something we do," Clint announced. "El Espectro may have finally made a mistake."

"What?" Barsa asked, totally confused.

"It's in the letter he left," the Gunsmith answered. "He mentions a town called Grajo. He says if you send someone there and just mention his name it'll get back to him. That means his headquarters must be located near Grajo."

"Clint," Woodland began, "If you can rescue my daughter, I'll pay you the five thousand dollars I was going to give el Espectro."

"I don't cotton to having my fee set by a kidnapper and a murderer," Clint said. "But I figure half that amount would be all right."

The congressman smiled—the first real smile he'd displayed since he'd met the Gunsmith. "I'll pay you the two thousand five hundred dollars before you leave."

"No," Clint told him. "Just five hundred now to cover expenses. You can pay me the rest when I return from Mexico."

"Thank you, Clint," Woodland said, tears of gratitude forming in his eyes.

The Gunsmith didn't like what he had to say next, but he had to say it anyway. "Don't thank me yet, Congressman," he warned. "I can't promise I'll be able to bring her back. Hell, I'm not even sure I'll be able to bring *myself* back."

FOUR

Joe Saunders examined his Winchester carbine with a toothless grin. "Golly, Mr. Adams," the hostler said. "You purely done this gun proud. If'n it ever looked so good before I done disremembered."

"I'm glad you like my work, Joe," Clint replied. "Just try to take better care of your firearms in the future. If the trigger spring breaks again, don't use the gun for a hammer or try to grow potatoes in the barrel. It'll make the next gunsmith's job a lot easier. Okay?"

"Sure, Mr. Adams." Joe nodded. Clint's sarcasm had gone so high over his head he didn't even catch its passing shadow.

"I'm going to take Duke with me for a little job down in Mexico," the Gunsmith explained. "I don't know how long I'll be gone, but I'd like to leave my wagon here. Pay you two weeks in advance to look after it. Fair enough?"

"Why course it is, Mr. Adams," Joe agreed. "In fact, you could just leave it here and pay me when you get back. . . ."

"Joe," Clint began as he produced his billfold, "the kind of job I'm going to do is the sort a fella doesn't always come back from."

"Oh"—the hostler nodded slowly—"well, if'n you

get killed down in Mexico, what do you want I should do with your wagon and possibles?''

"If I get killed down in Mexico, I don't really think I'll care," Clint replied. "Just see to it my belongings are safe and sound for the next two weeks and don't put anything up for auction before then."

"Whatever you say, Mr. Adams," Joe said as he accepted a generous advance from the Gunsmith.

"*Señor* Adams?" a voice called from the entrance of the livery stable.

Clint turned to see a small, thin man dressed in Levi's and a checkered shirt. He held a gray stetson in his hands and his head hung low. The man's complexion was dark and his button eyes looked as black as his hair.

"I am Juan Lopez," he explained. "*Señor* Woodland told me I would find you here."

"It's a pleasure to meet you," the Gunsmith said, reaching out to shake hands with the young Mexican. "Can I call you Juan?"

"Oh, *sí*!" The other man smiled as he pumped Clint's arm.

The Gunsmith returned the smile, although he didn't like what he saw. Juan Lopez was dressed like a cowboy, but his manner was that of a timid *peón* and he didn't carry a six-gun or even a sheath knife on his belt. Maybe he'd be a good guide and translator, but Clint suspected Juan would be about as useful in a gunfight as a crippled nun.

"Did Woodland explain what you're getting involved with?" he asked the Mexican youth.

"*Sí*," Juan answered. "I am to serve as your guide and interpreter in my native country of Mejico. I understand that this may be very dangerous because we are to rescue his daughter from el Espectro who is a very bad man, no?"

"A *very* bad man," Clint confirmed. "There's a good chance we'll be involved in some shooting before it's over. Could be one or both of us won't live to return to Texas. You realize that, Juan?"

The youth nodded. *"Sí, señor."*

"My name's Clint, okay?" the Gunsmith told him. "Now, we'll be heading toward a town called Grajo. Do you know where it is?"

"Sí, señ-Clint," Juan replied. "It is in the Sonora region near a desert called El Barriga del Diablo—the Devil's Belly. A very bad place with nothing but sand, rocks, snakes and Yaqui *indios*."

"But there are some towns, villages, a *rurale* post or two there?"

"Sí," the youth said. "Do you think *los rurales* will help us find *Señorita* Woodland and el Espectro?"

"I'm hoping the *rurales* will know more about the Ghost than the *federales*, Juan," Clint explained. "After all, the *rurales* are the regional police so they deal with a smaller area. The *rurales* in Sonora are closer to the situation which means they know more about it . . . I hope."

"Sometimes *los rurales* are not very good people, Clint," Juan said nervously, revealing a *peón's* distrust and fear of authority.

Clint knew enough about the *federales* and *rurales* to realize Juan's attitude wasn't without merit. Mexico had always been a turbulent country and had seen more than its share of revolutions, oppression and violence. The current government under Juarez was better than most, but Mexico still remained a state that favored politicians and aristocrats. Many of the men in uniform south of the border were no better than *bandidos* themselves.

"If the *rurales* aren't cooperative we'll talk to the people of the towns and villages," Clint said. "Somebody must know about el Espectro."

"*Sí*," Juan agreed without conviction.

"I'm getting my horse ready for the trail," Clint told him. "Why don't we meet at the general store and you can help me select the supplies we'll need?"

"As you say." The youth nodded. "I too must get my horse and maybe change my clothes for the trip. *Mejicanos* tend to speak more freely to other *mejicanos*. In Texas, I dress like a Texan, but I might do better to look like my countrymen when we go to Sonora."

"You know your people better than I do, Juan," Clint answered. "Do you have a gun?"

"I have a rifle," Juan said; he seemed embarrassed. "It is not much of a gun and I am not very good with it."

"What kind is it?" Clint asked.

"A Spencer carbine."

"One of those big fifty-two or fifty-four caliber cannons?" The Gunsmith rolled his eyes. "No wonder you're not very good with it. You can't weigh more than a hundred and twenty pounds, for God's sake. The recoil must beat hell out of your shoulder. We'll get you a Winchester or Henry saddle gun with ammunition in forty-four caliber. Now, have you ever used a pistol?"

"No, *señor* . . . Clint."

"Well, now is a poor time to teach you." Clint sighed. "You have a horse that's fit for some hard riding?"

"Oh, *sí*," Juan smiled. "I have a fine Appaloosa. Very strong and very fast."

"Good," the Gunsmith said. "We might have to outfit you with a new saddle, but your animal sounds okay. Take him over to the general store and I'll meet you there in ten minutes."

The young Mexican scurried away. Joe Saunders approached Clint and frowned. "How come you let that greaser call you by your first name when I gotta call you Mr. Adams?"

"You don't have to call me Mr. Adams," the Gunsmith replied. "Besides, I'm going to be sharing a lot of miles with that young fella and I want to be on good terms with him."

"I heard you say you was goin' after el Espectro." The hostler shook his head grimly. "If'n you'll take my advice, *Clint*"—he said the name with relish—"you'll forget all about tanglin' with that Mex devil."

"I'm not exactly looking forward to it, Joe," Clint admitted.

"You wanna know about el Espectro?" Joe began. "I can tell you where to find out all about him."

The Gunsmith turned to gaze at the aged hostler. Joe's expression was stern and his eyes wide, with a trace of fear visible in them.

"I'm listening, Joe."

"You can read about the dead man who rides a white stallion in the Book of Revelation," Joe replied in a solemn voice. "*I looked, and behold a pale horse: and his name that sat on him was Death.*"

FIVE

Past experience assured the Gunsmith that with ample time he could find any man, anywhere, no matter how elusive. Ask enough questions, grease enough palms with silver eagles, check enough leads and maybe ruffle enough folks' feathers and eventually you'll find your man—if he doesn't come looking for you first.

Time, however, was something Clint Adams didn't have. Neither did Marsha Woodland. If the girl was still alive the only chance she had was if Clint could find her quickly. El Espectro may have already arranged to sell her to a remote brothel in Central America. He certainly wouldn't hold her too long in the hopes his scheme would work.

The Gunsmith and Juan Lopez quickly packed their supplies in saddlebags and draped them across the backs of their horses. Clint bought Juan a new rifle, and as he'd guessed, the young Mexican also needed a new saddle, which the Gunsmith purchased as well. Clint was relieved to discover Juan had not exaggerated about his horse. The Appaloosa appeared quite fit and strong. Compared to Duke, the other animal seemed undersized and underfed, but most horses looked shabby next to the magnificent black Arabian.

They rode out of Brookstown before noon and crossed a wide ford in the Rio Grande into Mexico by dusk. Clint and Juan covered several miles before darkness made travel by horseback too hazardous. Galloping around after nightfall is a good way to break a horse's leg in a prairie-dog hole. Besides, the territory could well be inhabited by Yaqui or Apache Indians, many of whom migrated from Texas after the Comanches and the white-eyes pony soldiers had made life too difficult for their taste.

The two men set up camp on the Mexican prairie, which looked like any prairie one might find in the United States. Sand, rocks, cottonwoods and sagebrush don't differ much wherever they're found.

They camped near a cluster of boulders and began to unpack coffee, sourdough bread, beef jerky and canned tomatoes for dinner. While Clint fed and watered the horses, Juan collected greasewood for a fire. The Gunsmith gave Duke a rubdown with a tattered horse blanket when he noticed Juan poking about the boulders with a stick.

"Worried about rattlesnakes?" Clint asked.

"*Sí*," the youth admitted. "And scorpions and most of all, *el lagarto de cuentas*."

"What's that?" the Gunsmith inquired as he started the campfire.

"The beaded lizard," Juan explained. "It is similar to the gila monster native to Texas and New Mexico. The beaded lizard is also poisonous and it too has jaws of iron. The beaded lizard is more deadly than any serpent and when it bites you, it won't let go even if you cut its head off."

"Sounds like I wouldn't care to have one of them share my bedroll," Clint remarked, placing a blue metal coffeepot by the fire.

"The Yaqui Indians use the poison of *el lagarto de cuentas* on the heads of their war arrows," Juan continued as he joined Clint by the fire. "You get shot by a Yaqui arrow, you'll be dead for sure."

"Terrific," the Gunsmith muttered, glancing about the surrounding shadows. "Are the Yaqui very active in this area?"

"No." The youth shrugged. "This far north you might run into Apache, but we won't have to worry about Yaqui until we reach Sonora."

Clint turned to face Juan. "You realized we'd be traveling through hostile Indian territory and probably wind up in a shooting match with el Espectro and his gang. Why did you come, Juan?"

"*Señor* Woodland says he'll pay me five hundred dollars if I help you rescue his daughter. That is a lot of money, Clint. I have a wife and five children. Right now I can not provide for them too good, but I'll be able to give them more than we dared dream possible when I return home."

"Five hundred dollars." Clint shook his head. Woodland had offered him ten times that amount. "That's the price you put on your own life, Juan?"

"Risking my life for my family is something I gladly accept, Clint," Juan replied. "I was born a *peón* in a tiny village where no one could ever hope to rise above his station. In los Estados Unidos there are opportunities for anyone to better himself if he tries. I want my children to have those opportunities."

"Who will provide for your wife and kids if you don't come back, Juan?"

"I must return," the youth insisted. "What is your reason, Clint? Certainly, you are not simply attracted by the money. You do not have a wife and little ones, do you?"

"No," Clint answered. "But that doesn't mean I can't use some extra cash. I don't make much of an income by fixing folks' firearms, so Woodland's money will come in handy."

"But there is another reason, no?"

The Gunsmith nodded. "There's an innocent girl held captive by a man who seems to be part devil. Maybe she's already dead or maybe she's already been sold to a whorehouse in Colombia, but if she's still alive and I can help her, well . . . I'd just have a pretty hard time looking at my face in the mirror when I shaved if I didn't try."

"*Sí.*" Juan smiled. "You are a good man, Clint. A man of honor."

"Right now, I'm a pretty tired man," Clint declared. "Let's get some sleep. Tomorrow promises to be another long, hard day."

SIX

The Gunsmith and Juan Lopez awoke at dawn. They were in the saddle an hour later. Their journey continued into the monotonous miles of flat prairies of the Sonora desert region.

"We should reach Grajo by sundown," Juan remarked.

"We're not going to Grajo," Clint said as he removed a folded map from his shirt pocket.

"But how are we supposed to find el Espectro if we do not follow his instructions and go to Grajo?" the startled youth asked.

"Never play by another fella's rules if you have a better chance of beating him by making up your own," the Gunsmith declared. "The Ghost wants us to go to Grajo. That means it would be to *his* advantage if we did so. We're going to try to find him another way—one that he won't expect."

"Through the *rurales*?" Juan asked with a frown.

Clint nodded. "General Moreno gave me this map when I was in Mexico City. It has the locations of various *federale* and *rurale* posts throughout the country. The general wanted to be sure I could get help if I needed it on my way back to Texas. There's a *rurale* post, Fort Morales, about eight miles west of where I figure our present position to be."

"I still don't see what help the *rurales* can be. After all, they haven't been able to find el Espectro."

"Maybe they haven't had a good enough reason to really look for . . ."

Clint's sentence died before he could complete it when three figures appeared at the horizon. The trio of men on horseback also spotted the Gunsmith and Juan. They rapidly approached. Clint dropped his hand to the Colt on his hip and slipped the thong from its hammer in case he needed to draw the gun in a hurry. Juan slid his Winchester from its saddle boot. He whispered a prayer to the Holy Virgin as he chambered a round.

As the trio drew closer, Clint saw they wore uniforms and stovepipe riding boots similar to *federales*, but the horsemen didn't sport military caps. Their sombreros, with star-shaped badges pinned to the crowns, identified them as *rurales*.

"Well"—Clint grinned—"maybe we're in luck."

"*Buenos días*," a bearded figure with the chevrons of a sergeant on his sleeve, greeted. He waved at the Gunsmith and displayed a set of tobacco stained teeth as he smiled. "You are a *norteamericano*, no? I am *Sargento* Veaga. I speak English okay, no?"

"Better than my Spanish," Clint replied with a nod, but his hand didn't move from the grips of his Colt. The Mexican noncom's friendliness seemed false to the Gunsmith, who had learned never to assume too much at face value. "Perhaps you can help us, *Señor Sargento*."

"What you need, *amigo?*" Veaga still smiled. His hand rested on a button-flap holster on his belt.

"We're looking for Fort Morales," Clint explained.

He noticed the two soldiers with Veaga held rifles in their fists. One of them worked the lever to jack a shell into the breech.

"What good fortune!" Veaga declared. "We are from Fort Morales! Why you need to go there, *señor?* You attacked by *bandidos*, no?"

"No," Clint began, watching Veaga pry open his holster.

"Oh, *sí!*" the sergeant insisted. "Me and my *muchachos* we find you after the *bandidos* ambushed you here at this very spot." Veaga laughed. "Too bad they killed you, *gringo!*"

The *rurale* gestured at his men with one hand while the other fumbled for his pistol. Both privates swung their rifles toward Clint and Juan, bringing the buttstocks to their shoulders. Frightened and stunned by the unexpected aggression, Juan's shaky hands made an effort to bring his Winchester into play, although he realized his awkward response was too slow and the *rurales* would gun him down before he could hope to get off a shot.

Then the Gunsmith's Colt roared.

A .45 slug hit one of the *rurale* riflemen in the center of his chest, knocking him out of the saddle to die in a kicking heap on the ground. Clint's double-action revolver snarled a shred of a second later and the other *rurale* private's head recoiled violently when a bullet punched through it as though it were made of papier-mâché.

"*Cristo!*" Veaga cried in alarm and horror as he finally pulled his pistol from leather and tried to thumb back the hammer.

"*Adiós*," Clint muttered as he shot the sergeant in the forehead.

The sound of gunfire echoed on the wind, blending with the *thump* of Veaga's corpse hitting the ground. Juan Lopez stared at the three dead men in astonishment. Clint Adams calmly removed the spent cartridges from his Colt and replaced them with fresh shells.

"*Madre de Dios!*" the youth exclaimed. "I have heard tales of men who are fast and accurate with a *pistola*, but I never believed such a thing was possible!"

"Neither did they." Clint shrugged, patting Duke's neck. "Guess we'll just have to find Fort Morales on our own now."

Juan's mouth fell open in disbelief. "*Qué es esto? Mucho loco!* You just killed three *rurales* and you want us to just ride on to their post? What if *los rurales* find these bodies and figure out you shot them?"

"We'll know how the *rurales* will react to that news when we get to the fort," Clint replied. "We're taking *Sargento* Veaga and his *amigos* with us. Lucky their horses aren't gun-shy. I'm glad we don't have to waste time chasing after them. . . ."

"*Locura!*" Juan cried. "Insanity! You will get us both placed before a firing squad before sunset!"

"Don't be silly, Juan." The Gunsmith grinned. "Everybody knows executions are held at dawn."

SEVEN

"Hijo de la chigada!" Colonel Raul Morales snarled as he slammed his fist on the desk. "You dare to come into *my* fort with three of *my* men who you admit you killed and then ask *me* for help? *Gringo cochino!"*

Clint Adams and Juan Lopez stood in Morales's office. They'd surrendered their weapons when they'd entered the *rurale* post. Three soldiers then led them at gunpoint to the colonel's office. The troopers remained in the room with weapons held ready in case the *loco* Anglo tried to attack their commander with his bare hands.

"I don't like being insulted in any language, Colonel," Clint told Morales. "So why don't we both act civilized about this?"

"Civilized?" Morales rose up behind his desk. Almost a foot shorter than Clint, he glared up at the Gunsmith, his eyes wide with anger and amazement at the *gringo*'s attitude.

"You kill my men and then talk about being civilized?" he demanded. *"Bastardo del Diablo!* I'll have you shot for this! Horses will draw and quarter you! My men will use your body for bayonet practice!"

"Before you do anything to me," Clint said stiffly, "you'd better look at this."

He handed Morales a letter of commendation awarded to Clint Adams by el Presidente Juarez in recognition of his unselfish service to the government of Mexico upon returning a fortune in gold to the national treasury. Morales's face paled as he read the document. The colonel sank into his chair behind the desk.

"Uh . . . Tell me again how this thing happened, *Señor* Adams," Morales urged in a choked voice.

"You've heard it twice already," Clint replied. "Don't tell me you're all that surprised to hear Veaga and a couple of his men decided to use a patrol for a chance to moonlight as bandits. The greedy bastards figured Juan and I would be easy targets. They planned to kill and rob us and then let the local *bandidos* take the blame."

The Gunsmith watched Morales chew his lower lip nervously. Clint decided to give the colonel a chance to save face. He wanted the man's cooperation, and he wouldn't get it by humiliating him.

"I'm certain," the Gunsmith began, "this is not a surprise to you, *Coronel*. A good commander always knows his men and I'm sure you've had your eye on Sergeant Veaga in the past. You've probably suspected he was an unprincipled criminal in uniform, but until now, you didn't have enough evidence to deal with him. Right?"

"Oh, *sí*!" Morales agreed quickly. "I—I think I can even get Major Garfalo to state that I'd had Veaga and his scum under observation for months."

"I'm certain the major will support you, *Coronel*,"

Clint said with a straight face. "And may I congratulate you on your performance a moment ago?"

"Performance?" the bewildered Morales knitted his shaggy eyebrows.

"When you pretended to be outraged about the death of Veaga and his accomplices," the Gunsmith explained. "Quite convincing. You had me worried for a moment. Of course, you had to be certain I wasn't a *gringo* outlaw who was doing business with this corrupt sergeant. I commend your cleverness in forcing me to show you these documents to prove the value of my word."

"Uh . . . *sí*!" Morales nodded. "I—I hope I did not offend you, *Señor* Adams."

"Certainly not," Clint assured him. "Trust must be earned by strangers. A professional, such as yourself, cannot afford to leave anything to chance. I will be certain to mention you to General Moreno in Mexico City. I'll tell him about your shrewd judgment of men and your skilled command of this post as well as how you cooperated with me."

"You are too kind." Morales beamed. "You have done me a great service by helping me expose Veaga and his *cabróns*, so I will be pleased to assist you anyway I can."

"First," the Gunsmith began, "will you have your men return our weapons?"

The colonel immediately snapped fierce orders at his soldiers in rapid Spanish. The startled *rurales* handed Clint his gunbelt and hastily left the office. The Gunsmith winked at Juan Lopez, who was so amazed and relieved by the way Clint had rescued them from a firing squad, he looked as if he might faint.

"My friend Juan and I are on a mission," the Gunsmith told Morales. "A dangerous mission. We must find the *bandido* known as el Espectro."

Morales shook his head. "That will not be easy, *señor*. El Espectro is well named for he not only resembles a ghost in appearance, he can also vanish like a phantom as well."

"But there's nothing supernatural about the bullets he uses, *Coronel*," Clint insisted. "What can you tell me about this bandit?"

"Little that you don't already know," Morales admitted as he rose from his desk and approached a wall map. "We're fairly certain his camp must be somewhere here, in the desert called El Barriga del Diablo, which has to be one of the worst places on the face of the earth. We have a small post there, Fort Juarez, commanded by *Capitán* Garcia. He may be able to tell you more about el Espectro. However, this is Yaqui territory and *los rurales* must concentrate most of their efforts on dealing with the *indio* filth instead of *bandidos*. El Espectro is merely an annoyance compared to the Yaqui. And I must warn you to beware of those savages if you enter the Devil's Belly. There is no creature anywhere in the world that is more cruel or deadly than the Yaqui. Even the Apache fear them. Do not take this warning lightly, *Señor* Adams."

"I appreciate your help, *Coronel*," the Gunsmith replied. "And Juan and I will exercise the greatest caution in the Devil's Belly. Thank you, *Coronel*."

"*Vaya con Dios, Señor Adams*." Morales nodded.

The Gunsmith hoped the colonel was right and God would be with him in el Barriga del Diablo. Clint figured he'd need all the help he could get.

EIGHT

The Gunsmith was no stranger to deserts. He'd been to the Great Basin of Nevada, the Painted Desert of New Mexico and the formidable Imperial Valley of Southern California, but he'd never encountered a more bleak, lifeless stretch of territory than the Devil's Belly.

Oceans of sand extended for miles in every direction. The wind had formed ripples across the surface of the grainy brown sea. The only features to offer any relief to the sand were occasional clusters of rocks. Not even cactus or tumbleweed seemed able to survive in el Barriga del Diablo.

"Clint," a worried Juan Lopez began as he wiped his sweat-drenched brow with a damp neckerchief, "do you have any idea how much farther we have to go before we reach Fort Juarez?"

"About ten more miles," Clint replied. "I know. It seems like we've already ridden a hundred in this hellhole, but it's really not as bad as it seems."

"I hope you are right," Juan said without much conviction. "The desert can't be all like this, can it? I mean, if there are *rurales* and villages out here, there must also be water and food, no?"

"It'll get better, Juan," Clint promised—hoping he was right.

"Hey!" Juan thrust a finger at the horizon. "What's that?"

Clint used a hand to shield his eyes from the glare of the sun which sizzled overhead. He saw a couple of large gray and brown shapes in the distance. Heat vapors weaved across the objects and produced an eerie, flowing movement. At first, the rock formations appeared to be giant living creatures, but Clint sighed with relief when he realized the boulders weren't Mexican versions of the fabled "Clashing Rocks" of Greek mythology.

"Big excitement of the day, Juan," the Gunsmith declared. "We're approaching some rocks."

"I don't mean that, Clint," Juan insisted. "What's that thing between them? Looks like someone stuck a stick in the ground and put a ball on top of it."

The Gunsmith looked again and located the object. Juan's description was fairly accurate, although Clint thought the oval-shaped dome resembled a small melon more than a ball. As they drew closer, they noticed the "melon" was black on top. Then they saw why. Hair hung from the dome of the severed head perched on the stick. Its face was contorted in agony, jaws open in an eternal scream. Black horseflies clustered around the mouth and nose and the bloodied sockets that had once contained eyes.

"*Madre de Dios!*" Juan exclaimed.

The Gunsmith had encountered the barbarian nature of man before, yet he felt a cold shiver mount his spine when he gazed at the grisly head.

"The Yaqui sure have a unique way of marking their territory," Clint commented. He turned to Juan. "You want to go on?"

"No," the youth admitted. "But I will."

Both Duke and Juan's Appaloosa whinnied as they continued into el Barriga del Diablo. The animals smelled blood, death and horror. Clint and Juan soon discovered this for themselves. They found the decapitated corpse of the Yaqui's victim. The headless body lay by a rock formation, killed by an arrow which still protruded from its chest.

That was the good news.

Another man's corpse was sitting on the ground by the boulders. His arms were bound to three poles which formed an H-shaped frame. The Yaqui had cut off his nose, ears and lips. His eyeballs had been gouged out and a pile of ashes and grisly pulp revealed where the Indians had built a fire at the man's crotch.

Juan gasped, turned to one side and threw up.

Clint's stomach turned and he almost followed his partner's example. He was tempted to ask Juan if he wanted to turn back—and would have agreed if the youth said yes. Death was something the Gunsmith had seen more times than he could remember. He'd long ago accepted the fact that he'd die by violence, but a bullet crashing into one's heart or brain was one thing and a slow, painful death by torture was quite another.

"It is said," Juan began weakly, removing a canteen from the horn of his saddle, "that the Spanish taught the Yaqui how to do such things. Many of the *conquistadores* still followed the doctrines of the Holy Inquisition."

"The Yaquis don't need any more lessons," Clint remarked as he drew his Springfield carbine from its boot and worked the lever to chamber a round. "Hard to tell how long these fellas have been here. I don't really want to get a better look at them to make an educated guess."

"We'd better figure the Yaqui are still in the area, Clint," Juan advised. He washed his mouth out and spat the contents at the sand.

"Yeah," the Gunsmith nodded.

They continued to ride into el Barriga del Diablo . . . into the bowels of Hell.

NINE

The bleak, lifeless appearance of the Devil's Belly slowly changed. Patches of buffalo grass and an occasional cactus dotted the landscape. Yet this did not reduce the apprehension Clint and Juan felt as they rode across the desert sand.

An unnatural stillness dominated their nerve-racking journey. No birds sang in the distance, not even a lizard stirred on the ground, and the air refused to offer even a whisper of a breeze. Both men rode stiffly, reins held in one hand, rifles in the other. They constantly watched the surrounding rock formations for any trace of movement. Their ears strained to hear the slightest sounds of danger.

Their nerves were as taut as piano wire. Blood pulsed behind their ears sounding like the footfalls of bare feet. The rasping of their own breath was the snarl of the Grim Reaper about to pounce. Their heartbeats were bass drums playing a monotonous dirge inside their chests. Having seen the results of Yaqui torture, neither man could prevent his imagination from conjuring up mental displays of horror for the mind's eye.

The Gunsmith sensed someone's eyes following his every move—or was it merely another product of his imagination?

A sizzling missile of slender wood with a flint tip abruptly provided solid evidence of danger. Later, Clint would wonder what had alerted him. Perhaps he'd heard the creak of a taut bow bending as the archer drew back the string. Maybe he saw the blur of movement when the arrow was unleashed. Whatever the warning, it had been too faint to be registered consciously in his brain, but the Gunsmith's combat-sharpened reflexes responded anyway.

Clint suddenly dove from Duke's back as the arrow streaked over the saddle he had occupied a moment before. He kept his body loose when he hit the ground, rolling on a shoulder to rise up on one knee, his Springfield ready for battle.

A horrid shriek burst from the Appaloosa. Clint glanced at Juan's mount to see a feathered shaft jutting from the poor beast's neck. Juan cried out and kicked himself free of the stirrups, barely managing to jump from the saddle before the horse fell.

Clint whirled, swinging his carbine in the direction of the second archer. He spotted a Yaqui—small, painfully thin and naked except for a loincloth—standing at a natural barricade of stone. The Indian's chest was bisected by the front sight of Clint's Springfield. He squeezed the trigger and a .45 slug tore into the Yaqui's narrow chest. The brave screamed as his body was thrown backward into the rock wall before it slumped out of view.

A chorus of savage cries suddenly surrounded Clint and Juan. More Yaqui aggressors materialized from the rock formations. They moved swiftly, primitive weapons clenched in their bony fists, as they bobbed from rock to rock like lethal shadows on stone.

Clint jacked a fresh shell into the breech of his carbine while Juan crouched by the twitching body of his horse. Duke had been trained to respond to an assortment of dangerous situations and he was intelligent enough to always make the right decision even if he hadn't been taught to handle whatever came up. The big black galloped to the cover of the only rock formation that wasn't crawling with Yaqui. Duke's keen sense of smell had quickly located the best shelter and he was fast enough to reach it before the Yaqui archers could adjust their aim.

However, the Indians didn't fire at Duke. They only wanted to kill Clint and Juan. A Yaqui bowman rose up and fired a hasty missile at the Gunsmith. Clint immediately replied with his Springfield carbine. The arrow struck sand two feet in front of Clint, burying half its length in the ground. The Gunsmith's bullet smashed into human flesh. The Yaqui screamed and toppled forward, his body bouncing off boulders before it landed in a broken heap on the ground.

War cries bellowed in all directions and Yaquis seemed to spring up from the sand. Clint suddenly found himself surrounded by half a dozen murderous Indians who charged toward him, wielding lances and stone-headed tomahawks.

"Oh, shit!" he exclaimed, pumping the lever of his carbine.

Juan's Winchester cracked and a .44 slug smacked into a Yaqui, the force of the bullet knocking the Indian off his feet. The brave's body flopped on the ground, ignored by his comrades who kept heading toward the Gunsmith and his young Mexican partner.

Clint blasted another Springfield round into a

Yaqui's chest, the bullet burning a destructive tunnel through the Indian's heart before it ripped an exit hole between his shoulder blades. There wasn't time to chamber another shell in the carbine. The Yaqui were closing in quickly. Clint's left fist retained the Springfield, but his right streaked for the Colt .45 on his hip.

Two tomahawk-armed Yaqui continued to run toward Clint while a third stopped to cock his arm to prepare to throw his lance. The Gunsmith's double-action revolver spat flame twice and the two charging Yaqui were kicked into oblivion by .45 lead. Clint whirled as the spear rocketed toward him. It whistled past his left ear. Clint's Colt roared again and the third Indian's nose disappeared. The bullet sliced through his brain and popped open the back of the Yaqui's skull.

The last Yaqui assailant stood over the screaming figure of Juan Lopez. He'd driven the flint point of his lance into the young Mexican's right side until the stone blade caught on the bones of Juan's ribcage. When the Yaqui saw Clint shoot down his fellow tribesmen, he yanked the spear from Juan's ravaged flesh and desperately hurled it at Clint's back.

The Gunsmith pivoted, raising the Springfield carbine in his left fist. The barrel swung into the airborne lance, deflecting it in midair. Astonished and terrified, the Yaqui's jaw fell open. Clint's Colt snarled and a .45 round entered the Indian's open mouth. The brave was dead before he hit the ground.

Clint hurried to Juan's inert form and knelt beside his wounded partner. Still glancing about for more Yaqui aggressors, Clint placed two fingers against Juan's neck, searching for a pulse.

"I am not yet dead, *amigo*," the youth announced.

His voice was remarkably steady and clear for a man who'd been ripped open from hip to ribcage by sharp stone. The wound was terrible and blood gushed across Juan's shirt and trousers. Clint realized the youth was already as good as dead.

"You take it easy, Juan," he said. "Let me clean and bandage this and—"

"And I will die anyway," Juan stated calmly. "I am sorry I didn't do so good against the Yaqui. . . ."

"You did fine, Juan," Clint assured him. "You saved my life."

"Maybe." Juan smiled thinly. "But I won't be able to help you now. Guess I haven't been so good as a guide or translator. . . ."

"I've been honored to have you by my side," the Gunsmith told him.

"You are a fine man, Clint." Juan nodded. "Maybe you do me a favor?"

"Just name it."

"If . . . When you get back to Texas . . ."

"I'll see that your family gets the five hundred dollars Woodland promised to pay you," Clint assured him, guessing what Juan wanted. "In fact, I'll see to it they get at least a thousand. They'll be well taken care of. You have my word, *amigo*."

"That is good," Juan said.

Both men were silent for almost a full minute. Clint cradled Juan's head in one arm and held him gently, waiting for the youth to die. He wouldn't abandon Juan in these last moments of life. He owed the boy that much.

"You know," Juan began, his eyes gazing up at the

sky, "I didn't think it would be like this when I died. It doesn't hurt too much now and it really isn't too bad. . . ."

Then he said, "Clint, I see something. I can't describe it, but it is beautiful." He smiled. "Death is . . . *muy bello, amigo. Muy* . . ."

Then Juan Lopez quivered gently and died.

TEN

The Gunsmith buried Juan. He broke a Yaqui lance in two and tied the pieces together to form a crude wooden cross which he hammered into the grave for a marker.

"Well, God," he began as he stood by the grave, "you don't hear much from me. Maybe that's not good and maybe it's just as well. I don't know, but I don't want to talk about me anyway. I could say that Juan Lopez was a good man and he deserves salvation, but I figure that's up to You, God. Could say he loved his family and died bravely, but I reckon You know about that. Guess all I can say is Juan's had a long hard ride and I hope he finds some peace now."

Two hours later, Clint Adams found Fort Juarez. *Rurale* sentries saw the Gunsmith approach on foot, leading Duke by the reins. The great wooden gates opened and three uniformed figures met Clint at the threshold. A young officer with a sleek ferret face and a sly smile greeted him with a formal bow.

"I assume you are a *norteamericano*," he said. "Even if you speak *español*, please allow me to practice my English. I am *Teniente* . . . Lieutenant Santiago Sanchez. Who might you be, *señor*?"

"My name is Clint Adams," the Gunsmith replied hoarsely. "I wish to speak with the post commander, *Capitán* Garcia."

"I am certain the captain will be honored to meet you," Sanchez stated with poorly concealed sarcasm. "I will take you to him."

The *rurale* post was considerably smaller than Fort Morales, but other than that, the two installations looked very similar. Adobe wall surrounded the post, which consisted of simple structures that served as barracks for the enlisted men and an officers' billet. Horses were penned in a corral and the mess hall was a small enclosed kitchen surrounded by benches.

Sanchez led Clint to the headquarters building. *Capitán* Garcia sat behind a mistreated old desk, reading a dog-eared copy of *Uncle Tom's Cabin*. The post commander gazed up at Clint and Sanchez as they entered his office.

"*Capitán*," Sanchez began, "this is Clint Adams who has come all the way from los Estados Unidos to speak with you."

"Save your rudeness for the men, Lieutenant," Garcia replied. His English was flawless, the accent more New England than Mexico. "They have to respect your rank."

Sanchez merely shrugged in response.

Garcia rose from his chair. He was tall for a Mexican, almost the same height as the Gunsmith. Garcia was an impressive man, darkly handsome with a trim black mustache and deep-set eyes under dense black brows. His uniform was neat and barely wrinkled. The captain extended a hand to Clint.

"A pleasure to meet you, Adams," he said, shaking

hands solemnly. "It is rare to encounter a visitor from the North in this place. How may I help you?"

The Gunsmith told Garcia about el Espectro and Marsha Woodland. He explained how he and Juan had come to rescue the girl and about Juan's death at the hands of the Yaqui.

"Without a guide or translator," Clint concluded, "I'm at a disadvantage, but I still have a job to do and I'd appreciate any help you can give me, *Capitán*."

"Looking for el Espectro is like trying to capture the wind." Garcia sighed as he fished a black cheroot out of his pocket. "We have tried to find that white-skinned demon many times, but we've never even come close to success."

He struck a match and lit the cigar before he continued. "All we really know is el Espectro and his men are somewhere out there"—he cocked his head toward a window—"in the Devil's Belly. Occasionally, the Ghost will raid one of the local villages. The *peónes* have no real valuables, but el Espectro takes what he can find—food, water, alcoholic drinks and prisoners."

"Prisoners?" Clint raised his eyebrows. "He kidnaps *peónes*? Why?"

"Perhaps we would know if he ever released a captive." Garcia shrugged. "El Espectro and his men often abduct young men and women, for what reasons we can only guess. The women probably serve an obvious purpose, but the men . . . Well, some of the superstitious *peónes* believe el Espectro is an evil spirit. They whisper his name in terror and place crosses made of salt on the ground to try to ward him away. They think he might be a *caníbal* who gains power by devouring his victims' flesh . . . their hearts and brains, perhaps even their souls."

"Have you ever tried to surprise the Ghost when he comes ahaunting with his gun-toting ghouls?" Clint inquired.

"Oh, yes." Garica nodded. "But he has never arrived when we've done so. El Espectro seems to be able to sense the presence of his enemies. As you can see, this is not a large post. I do not have many men under my command and the Yaqui, such as the savages you encountered today, are more of a threat than the *bandidos*. Thus, I have not been able to station men at villages for months simply to wait for el Espectro to return. I'm certain your cavalry would not send a company of soldiers to protect a town from a gang of outlaws if they had to contend with a Sioux uprising."

"Towns in the United States have lawmen and most citizens own guns and know how to use them," Clint replied. "The James boys and the Younger brothers once tried to raid Northfield and they got shot up pretty bad before they ran out of town with their tails between their legs."

"Well"—Garcia drew on his cheroot—"in Mexico most *peónes* do not own guns and we don't want them to. We can't trust them to use weapons only to defend themselves against bandits. Rabble-rousers are always trying to incite revolution in my country."

"I'm sure your government knows what's best for them," Clint said dryly. *Maybe if the peónes weren't treated like dirt you wouldn't have to worry about revolutions*, he thought. "Well, if the *rurales* can't tell me how to find el Espectro, maybe I should talk to the *peónes*."

"Then I know where you should go," Garcia declared. "The village of San José was raided by el Espectro less than a week ago. May I suggest you talk with the priest there? Father Tomás Rameriz is a remarkable man. He is a blind man, yet he sees into the hearts of his people better than any *padre* I know. He is poor, but he received a fine education. He is a scholar and a linguist who speaks English, French and of course Latin, as well as Spanish."

Clint nodded in agreement. "Thanks for all your help, Captain. Now, if you'll tell me how to get to San José . . ."

"It will soon be dark, Mr. Adams," Garcia said. "You are welcome to spend the night here. You can continue your mission in the morning after you've eaten and slept . . . and perhaps, after you've considered the folly of your actions. Then you may decide to return to Texas."

"You don't think I'll find the Ghost?" the Gunsmith asked.

"Perhaps you will," Garcia replied grimly. "But to find el Espectro is to find Death, my friend."

ELEVEN

Clint Adams enjoyed the hospitality of Captain Garcia's post and ate a satisfying meal of *carne de carnero*, chili and tortillas with plenty of *cerveza* to wash it down. He saw to Duke's food and water and made certain the horse would be comfortable. Then Garcia escorted Clint back to his office where he'd set up a cot for the Gunsmith. Clint placed his weapons within arm's reach and gratefully went to sleep.

The following morning, two hours after dawn, the Gunsmith rode from Fort Juarez. He and Duke were refreshed and ready for the trail—or at least, as ready as anyone could be to journey into el Barriga del Diablo.

Captain Garcia's directions to the village of San José had been descriptive and accurate. Clint watched for various landmarks—a stone butte with a flat top, a snake-shaped arroyo, a boulder that resembled a buffalo's head—and steered Duke into another direction when he encountered them, recalling Garcia's instructions.

Clint arrived at San José before noon. The village was small with tiny houses made of adobe brick with reed-patched roofing. The church, a modest building with a wooden cross nailed above the entrance, was the largest structure in San José.

Scrawny chickens and goats wandered about the village. Four young men were working in a cornfield. When they saw Clint, they immediately put down their hoes and removed their sombreros to solemnly stare at the stranger. A pair of old women who had been grinding corn into meal also saw the Gunsmith and hastily retreated into the nearest hut.

"*Buenos días*," Clint greeted. "*Yo soy pacífico hombre. Comprende?*"

Although he'd assured the *peónes* he was a man of peace, they didn't seem to believe him. The Gunsmith sighed.

"*Dónde está el Padre Rameriz, por favor?*" he inquired.

"Here I am, *señor*," a deep, pleasant voice replied.

Clint turned to see a well-built man dressed in a patched cassock, who stood at the open door of the church. His jet black hair was streaked with silver. Clint guessed the priest to be in his mid-forties, a few years older than himself. Father Rameriz held a stave in his fist, the tip touching the edge of the top step to his church. The priest's forehead was high and his mouth turned up at the corners, suggesting a ready smile. His sightless eyes were milky white, yet they seemed to express intelligence and a kindly nature.

"My name's Clint Adams, Father," the Gunsmith explained as he swung down from Duke. "I was told you might be able to help me."

"To help others is part of the obligation we owe to God as good Christians and to ourselves as civilized men," Father Rameriz replied, cocking his head as he listened to Clint's approaching footfalls. "May I ask who advised you to seek me out, my son?"

"*Capitán* Garcia," Clint answered, mounting the steps to the church.

"Garcia?" Rameriz frowned for a moment. "The *rurales* are not popular with *peónes*, Clint. God loves all His children, but some, like the *rurales*, seem to deserve it less than others."

"How do you figure el Espectro rates with the Almighty?" Clint asked.

The priest's expression darkened. "I cannot speak for God, but I doubt that el Espectro and his followers deserve anything from Our Holy Father except eternal damnation—which I suspect they shall receive when their time of Judgment arrives."

Rameriz turned to enter his church, the stave guiding his way with ease. Clint followed the priest inside. Rows of wooden pews faced an altar and pulpit at the opposite side of the room. Tarnished copper candlesticks were positioned at both sides of the altar, but there were no collection plates in view. A wooden crucifix hung on the wall above the altar.

"Since you are a *norteamericano*," Father Rameriz began, "I assume you have a very strong reason to come to Sonora in search of el Espectro, no?"

Clint confirmed this and explained how he had been hired to locate the bandit leader and rescue Marsha Woodland. Father Rameriz listened, occasionally nodding as he led Clint to a door behind the pulpit.

"If I could help you in this task," the priest said, opening the door, "I would gladly do so, but I do not see how I can be of assistance, my son."

Rameriz and Clint entered the priest's chambers, which consisted of a small room with a cot, a bookcase, two cabinets and a chess set on a small table with two chairs.

"Garcia told me this village was recently attacked by the bandits," Clint said.

"*Sí*," the priest admitted as he felt for the handle of

a cabinet door and opened it. "El Espectro and his band rode in and ordered the villagers to give them food and water. This has happened before, so no one was very surprised or even disturbed by their demands."

Rameriz reached inside the cabinet and brought out a bottle of red wine and two clay cups. "But this time," he continued, "the *bandidos* took more than food and drink. They kidnapped two young women and three young men."

"El Espectro certainly wouldn't plan to collect ransom for *peónes*," Clint mused. "Why'd he take them?"

"I do not know, my son," the priest replied. "He might abduct the women to serve as playthings for his *bandidos* and merely take the male prisoners to confuse and frighten us. Or . . . perhaps it is as some believe and el Espectro is a messenger of the Devil, sent to remind us that evil is real and alive."

"Do you think he's an evil spirit, Father?"

Rameriz carefully poured wine into the cups, measuring the portions by judging the increased weight of the cups. "I do not know if el Espectro is an evil spirit," the priest declared. "But he is certainly an evil man. Of course, I have never seen el Espectro, but my people tell me the Ghost indeed resembles a corpse. They say his face looks like a death mask and his skin is as white as a cloud."

"El Espectro—whoever he might really be—is obviously playing his dead man act to the hilt in order to take advantage of the *peónes'* superstitions," Clint stated. "It sounds like he powders his face like an actor to create that appearance. That's your evil spirit, Father—just another *bandido*, who wears clown makeup on his raids."

"I'm sure you are right, my son," Father Rameriz began, handing Clint a cup of wine. "But I have heard the voice of el Espectro. It is a hollow voice, like the wind rasping among headstones in a graveyard."

"Thanks for the drink, Father," Clint said.

"You are welcome, my son," Rameriz nodded. "Do you play chess, Clint?"

"Yes," the Gunsmith replied.

"Then you are even more welcome." The priest smiled.

With a cup of wine in one hand and his cane in the other, Rameriz approached the chess set. "Would you care to play a game, Clint?"

"All right," the Gunsmith agreed, wondering how a blind man could play chess.

When he got a closer look at the chess set, he found the answer. Each hand-carved piece was marked with raised dots on its back. *Braille*, Clint realized. Father Rameriz could thus identify chessmen by rank and color simply by touching a piece. Every other square on the checkerboard was slightly raised, allowing the priest to move his men by touch.

"This is quite a chess set," Clint remarked as he sat behind the white army.

"So you've already noticed it has some unusual features." Rameriz smiled, positioning himself at the black army. "If pride is a sin, then I am guilty for I can not help feeling pride in my chess set."

"You came up with the idea?" Clint asked.

"When my eyes began to fail and I knew I would soon be blind," Rameriz explained, "I made this set. I carved the figures and the board so I would still be able to play chess after I lost my sight."

"Captain Garcia told me you're a remarkable man, Father," Clint stated. "He didn't exaggerate."

"I am just a priest, Clint." Rameriz shrugged. "I had the advantage of a fine education, but I wasn't a very good priest when I was an intellectual. I was conceited, arrogant and impatient with the shortcomings of others. Yet, after I lost my sight, I devoted myself to the poor, to help them not only spiritually but also to educate them. Most *peónes* are illiterate, but everyone in San José can read and write. Have you moved yet, Clint?"

"Oh, yeah," the Gunsmith said. "Queen's knight to bishop three."

"I have taught English to many of the villagers as well," the priest continued as he moved his king's pawn forward. "I'd like to see more of them move to your country where they'll have a chance to better themselves. Mexico is a better country under el Presidente Juarez, but I fear his reign may not last for long. Yet, if enough of my people see what your government is like, a true republic with a constitution that grants its citizens rights at birth, then we may be able to improve Mexico in time."

"I moved the king's knight to bishop three," Clint told him.

"So, you put your knights toward the center of the board where you can make the most of their evasive L-shaped pattern of movement." Rameriz nodded. "A good defensive tactic, my son. When will you go back to your great nation north of the border?"

"When I've finished my job here," Clint replied. "You seem to admire the United States, Father. Why don't you move there?"

"Because this is my country." The priest moved a bishop forward. "And because here is where I am needed, my son."

"*Padre Rameriz!*" an excited voice shouted from beyond the chamber door.

"*Entra, mi niño,*" the priest called in reply.

A button-eyed *peón* appeared at the entrance of Rameriz's quarters. He held his sombrero in his hands as he breathlessly spoke a rapid sentence in Spanish. All that Clint could catch of the words were "el Espectro."

"The men in the fields have just seen a large group of horsemen approaching the village," Rameriz explained to Clint. "They recognized the leader. El Espectro will be here in another minute or two."

TWELVE

"I'm looking for the Ghost," Clint remarked. "But I didn't expect to meet him under these circumstances."

"This is certainly no time to try to fight him," Father Rameriz declared. "He has too many men with him."

The priest quickly snapped an order in Spanish to the *peón* who nodded in reply and bolted from the church. Father Rameriz rose from his chair and turned to Clint.

"I told Luis to fetch you a *sombrero* and *serape*. It isn't a very good disguise, but it will make you less conspicuous than *norteamericano* clothing, no?"

"Good idea," Clint agreed. "What about my horse? It's bound to draw the bandits' attention."

"Bring the animal into the church." Rameriz smiled. "This is God's house and your horse is one of His creations. I'm certain He will not object to its visit under the circumstances."

"What if the *bandidos* search the church?" Clint asked. "They'll kill you, Father."

"This is a chance we must take, my son." Rameriz shrugged. "But I doubt that el Espectro and his men have any interest in a church which they know contains no gold or silver candlesticks or even a poor box. Now hurry and get your horse."

Clint led Duke up the steps and inside the church. Luis, the *peón*, appeared again with a serape and sombrero. Before the Gunsmith could thank him, the young Mexican had again bolted from the church.

As Clint donned the blanketlike poncho and battered straw headgear, he heard the thundering roar of approaching horse hooves. He patted Duke's muzzle and whispered to the big gelding to be quiet. Then he drew his Springfield carbine from the saddle boot and waited.

Father Rameriz stood at the entrance of the church while Clint and Duke remained behind the door out of sight. The Gunsmith, however, still saw enough via the space between the door and its frame to know what kind of men the new arrivals on horseback were.

The Gunsmith had encountered *bandidos* before and he recognized the breed immediately. Brutal, hard men, armed to the teeth with guns, knives and bandoliers, the bandits sat arrogantly on their mustang horses and gazed contemptuously at the villagers of San José. The *bandidos*—skinny or fat, late teens or early forties—were otherwise alike—bearded, dirty, unprincipled savages that resembled the wild animals they had become.

All, that is, except the incredible figure mounted on a great white stallion who led them.

The bandit chief's horse was indeed magnificent, almost as beautiful and large as Duke. The animal was as white as Clint's gelding was black. As white as the man who rode it.

The descriptions of the Ghost had not been an exaggeration. He was clad in black trousers and boots with a black hooded cowl over his head. Yet, the man's face was visible. Lean, gaunt and the color of chalk, his features could have been carved in marble. The Gunsmith had heard about el Espectro, but he wasn't prepared for what he saw . . . or what he *felt*. The man was indeed more than a common hill bandit. He was a sinister force in human form.

The phantom addressed the village of San José. Although Clint could not understand most of the words, he detected a smooth Castilian accent in el Espectro's Spanish which suggested he'd received an expensive formal education. Clint also heard the slow, deep rumble of the Ghost's terrible voice. He could not suppress the cold shiver that traveled along his spine.

God in Heaven, what have I gotten myself into? Clint thought. *That man out there—whatever he is—is unlike anything I've taken on in the past.*

The Gunsmith tried to get as good a view of el Espectro as possible without exposing himself. He noticed something no one had mentioned before. The Ghost wore eyeglasses, a pair of thick spectacles with dark smoked lenses. What startled Clint the most was the fact that el Espectro's alabaster white skin *did not* appear to be a simple cosmetic trick. Even the man's bony, long-fingered hands were as pale and bloodless as a corpse.

After what seemed like hours of nerve-racking tension, el Espectro gestured to his men. Clint then heard the rumble of hooves gallop from San José. He was still listening to the sound gradually growing dimmer when Father Rameriz clutched his arm. The blind man leaned close to Clint as he spoke softly.

"You must remain here, my son," the priest whispered. "The danger is not yet over. One of the *peónes* the bandits captured from our village, a girl, has managed to escape from el Espectro's lair. I told them she is not here—which, in truth, she is not—but for one awful moment, I feared el Espectro would order his men to search the village for the girl."

"Guess I'm glad I don't understand Spanish," Clint said.

"Listen, my son," Rameriz urged. "El Espectro left three of his men behind in case the girl returns to San José. They are stationed right outside the church. You must be quiet and wait. *Comprende*?"

"I understand, Father," Clint assured him. "And I'll wait . . . for a while."

THIRTEEN

The Gunsmith and Duke stood behind the door of the church while long minutes dragged by. Clint listened to the three *bandidos* el Espectro had left behind. The trio shouted commands in Spanish. Clint understood enough of it to realize the bandits were ordering the *peónes* to bring them food and water.

Clint heard a woman squeal in pain, followed by the cruel laughter of the trio. His hand touching the grips of his Colt, the Gunsmith leaned forward to peer through the crack of the door. Three filthy figures clad in dusty clothes, sombreros and ammo belts crisscrossing their chests, stood in the center of the village. The woman, a homely middle-aged *peón*, ran from the bandits.

Apparently, they hadn't really harmed her, but Clint still had to remind himself that if he confronted the bandits—which he sorely wanted to do—gunshots might be heard by el Espectro and the others, who would certainly return to investigate the sounds. He had to wait until the Ghost and his crew were out of earshot before he could take any action against the three bandits.

Father Rameriz took the incident in stride. He'd encountered *bandidos* before and this wasn't the first time they'd terrorized his village. The priest carried a broom, using it as a cane to feel his way to the door. Locating the threshold, he stepped outside and began to sweep the steps of the church.

"*Padre!*" a bandit snarled, gesturing at the priest although he knew Rameriz to be blind. "*Venga usted, Padre!*"

Father Rameriz, using the broom to guide his way, obeyed the order and approached the three men. "*Qué deseas, señor?*" he inquired.

The Gunsmith listened to the *bandidos* laugh as they uttered sentences in Spanish, unintelligible to Clint. He saw the *bandidos* surround Rameriz. They poked and shoved him contemptuously, but the priest submitted passively to the abuse. One of the Mexican outlaws, a beefy, bearded beast, wrenched the broom from Rameriz's grasp and broke it over his knee.

Clint stiffened when he saw the *bandido* grab the priest's cassock in his fist. He pulled Rameriz close, their faces almost touching. The bandit growled something at Rameriz and shoved him forcibly. Another bandit extended a leg and the priest tripped over it. He fell to the ground to the amusement of his tormentors.

Damn it! Clint thought. *This has gone far enough!*

The stocky bandit stepped closer to Father Rameriz as the priest got to his hands and knees and started to rise. A boot stamped into his side and knocked Rameriz on his face. The bandit chuckled and said something that ended with "*Dios.*" Rameriz, still on all fours, seemed to stiffen with anger.

With a vicious smile on his bearded face, the beefy brute growled another sentence at Rameriz. The priest did not move or speak. The *bandido* shouted something and Father Rameriz raised his head and spat at him.

BANDIDO BLOOD

"Bastardo de Dios!" the bandit bellowed.

He slashed a boot at the priest's head, but Tomás Rameriz either heard or sensed the movement of the attacking leg before the kick could connect. Moving with surprising speed, the priest's arms rose, blocking the kick. The bandit cried out in alarm as Rameriz grabbed the man's leg and twisted it, throwing his tormentor off balance.

The *bandido* hit the ground hard and Rameriz, holding the leg with one hand, hammered his fist into the brute's groin. The bandit shrieked in pain. The priest punched him in the crotch again and the other bandits cursed and reached for Rameriz.

"You pieces of taco-vomit want a fight?" Clint Adams declared as he stepped from the door of the church. "Here it is."

The two *bandidos* immediately forgot the priest and swung around to face the Gunsmith, their hands streaking for their holstered pistols. Clint's Colt was already in his hand, the hammer cocked, his finger on the trigger.

Almost casually, he shot one of the bandits in the face. A grisly halo of shattered skull fragments and brains burst from the back of the man's head. His partner was still clawing at his sidearm when Clint pumped two .45 slugs into his chest.

The Gunsmith trained his pistol on the third *bandido*, but the brute didn't present a threat. He'd passed out from the ball-busting Father Rameriz had delivered with his fists. Clint approached, his gun still held ready.

"You okay, Father?" Clint asked.

"Sí," Rameriz nodded, his face still clouded by anger. *"Hijo del Diablo!"* he snarled, addressing the

unconscious bandit. *"Suciedad boca! Mierda!"*

Clint whistled softly, recognizing enough words to know Rameriz was using some pretty strong language for a priest. He knelt beside the man Rameriz had rendered senseless and removed his gunbelt. Then he frisked the bandit for holdout weapons, finding a rusty derringer and a boot knife.

"I am sorry for my outburst," Rameriz told him. "And I ask God to forgive me for my loss of temper and violence this day."

"I can't speak for the Almighty, but I'm not offended," the Gunsmith assured him. "What did this fella say that set you off like a keg of blackpowder?"

"This . . . man," Rameriz began, still struggling to control his anger. "He told me to kneel before him. He said, 'You worship God, priest? I now hold the power of life or death over you.' He told me he was thus my god and ordered me to worship him. Such blasphemy!"

"He's probably pretty sorry he made that remark, Father." Clint glanced at the stunned *bandido* who groaned softly and began to massage his battered crotch. "Especially since he'll be saying his Hail Marys in soprano for a while."

FOURTEEN

The *bandido* regained consciousness to discover the muzzle of a .45 Colt pointed at his face. Clint Adams cocked the hammer.

"If you don't speak English," the Gunsmith said in a cold, flat voice, "I'm going to kill you, fella."

He didn't really intend to shoot the man in cold blood, but it was a sure fire way to find out about his linguistic abilities.

"*Cristo!*" the bandit rasped, still holding his genitals with one hand. "*Sí!* I speak English!"

"What's your name, goat turd?" Clint asked.

"Pedro Castro," the bandit replied through clenched teeth. He glanced about for his companions.

"They're dead, Castro," Clint explained. "I killed them and if you don't do exactly what I tell you to do, I'll kill you too. Understand?"

"*Sí.*" The *bandido* nodded. "I understand."

"Get up," Clint ordered as he stepped back, still holding his gun on Castro.

The bandit obeyed, wincing from the pain that branched out from his groin. Father Rameriz approached with his stave in one hand, a coil of rope in the other.

"You've been unconscious for quite a while and el Espectro didn't return, so he must have been too far away to hear the gunshots when I killed your friends," Clint told Castro. "So don't expect the bandit cavalry to arrive. Now, hold out your hands so Father Rameriz can tie your wrists together. Don't try anything, fella, or I'll shoot off what's left of your *cajones*."

The priest firmly bound Castro's wrists together and stepped back to join Clint. The bandit's eyes dripped venom as he glared at them. Then his eyes widened with surprise when he saw one of the *bandido* mustangs and the beautiful black Arabian hitched to a rail by the church.

"That's right, Castro," Clint said. "You and I are going for a little ride. If you didn't have to ride a horse, I would have tied your hands behind your back. So don't get any notions that I'm an *estúpido gringo* who's going to make a mistake that'll allow you to jump him after we leave here. Give me half a reason and I'll shoot you in both kneecaps and leave you in the desert with nothing but snakes, scorpions and the Yaqui for company."

"The desert?" Castro wrinkled his brow. "You mean the Devil's Belly?"

"That's where el Espectro's headquarters is, right?" Clint said. "You're going to lead me there, *chico*."

Castro smiled. "To find el Espectro is to find Death. I will be happy to take you to him, *Señor* . . . ?"

"Adams," the Gunsmith supplied. "Now, get your ass on that horse and don't touch that black gelding. He'll bite your hand off if you try."

The bandit continued to obey orders. He groaned when he straddled the saddle on the back of the mustang. Castro didn't try to gallop away, aware Clint could have easily shot him off the horse before he could ride beyond pistol range. The Gunsmith addressed Father Rameriz without taking his eyes or his Colt from Pedro Castro.

"Thanks for everything, Father," he said. "If I can liberate any of your people and help them return to San José, I will."

"I know," the priest replied, placing a hand on Clint's shoulder. "May God go with you, my son."

"I sure hope so, Father," Clint remarked. "I'd sure hate to be riding through the Devil's Belly with just a snake like Castro for company."

FIFTEEN

"El Espectro don't like *gringos*, Adams," Pedro Castro declared as he and the Gunsmith rode through the blistering, barren desert of el Barriga del Diablo. "You know what he did one time when we caught a *gringo* lawman near El Paso? He cut off the man's pecker and stuffed it in his mouth."

"Thanks for the suggestion," Clint said, cocking back the brim of his straw sombrero with a thumb. He still wore the hat and serape in order to look less conspicuous. "I'll remember it if I get tired of listening to you talk."

"Oh, you are a tough *hombre*, Adams." The bandit nodded. "But no man is tough when he meets el Espectro. He is not like other men."

Clint clucked his tongue against the roof of his mouth. "Save that crap for the *peónes*, Castro."

"But it is true, Adams," the bandit insisted. "El Espectro can read your thoughts by gazing at your face. He can drain a man's strength with his voice or crush your skull with his bare hands."

"Can he also cure warts?" the Gunsmith sneered, but in fact he was disturbed by Castro's claims because the bandit seemed genuinely to believe in el Espectro's supernatural powers. "Tell me, Castro. Why'd you give that priest such a hard time back in San José?"

"I hate priests," the bandit declared. "The Catholic church has been the curse of Mexico ever since *los conquistadores* came and destroyed the Aztec empire in the name of Christ."

"I bet old Mr. Ghost told you that," Clint muttered.

"Laugh if you wish, *gringo*." Castro smiled. "But el Espectro has outwitted all his opponents because he can see what lies in the future and what his enemies plan. None of us fully understands him, but we don't need to. He is more than a man. You will see this for yourself."

"I already saw him." Clint shrugged. "A skinny fella who looks like he got hit with a bag of flour. What makes him so special?"

"The best way I can describe it is to tell you what he once said," Castro replied, his voice as solemn as a preacher reciting Scripture. "There is Life and there is Death, and el Espectro is the bridge between them."

"Jesus," Clint muttered. "You idiots are following a bleached-out medicine man."

"You'll see, *gringo!*" the bandit hissed, raising his bound wrists. His fists were clenched so tightly the knuckles were white. "You'll see."

"Shut up!" the Gunsmith snapped. He turned in the saddle and glanced about at the surrounding rock formations. "I heard something."

"What?" Castro inquired nervously.

"I'm not sure. Could have been stone shifting on sand, or footsteps. . . ." Clint moved his hand to the holstered Colt on his hip.

"Could be the Yaqui," Castro remarked fearfully.

Clint continued to scan the rocks as he strained his ears, listening for a telltale sign to reveal the location of whoever or whatever was trailing them. He was certain he felt eyes watching his every move.

BANDIDO BLOOD

"Better give me a gun, Adams," the bandit urged.

"That's pretty good, Castro," Clint sneered. "You know any other jokes?"

"You can't fight them by yourself. . . ."

"I thought I told you to shut up," the Gunsmith growled.

"Do you know what the Yaqui do to their victims?" Castro demanded. He raised his hands to his mouth and began to bite at the ropes.

"Stop that or I'll—" Clint began.

The sound of footsteps rushing toward him quickly drew the Gunsmith's attention to a figure near a cluster of boulders. A small, slim girl clad in a tattered white dress ran from the rocks.

"*Señor!*" she called hoarsely. "*Señor*, help me, *por favor!*"

Clint stared at her in astonishment. Not only was he stunned to encounter a girl alone in the Devil's Belly, but she was beautiful as well. Her long, raven black hair swayed across her shoulders as she ran and her oval face featured a wide sensuous mouth and huge, dark eyes.

The little Mexican beauty's figure was just as good as her face. Although barely an inch over five feet tall, her legs were perfectly proportioned with her compact body. A rip in her dress revealed a round breast with a small brown nipple that seemed to stare at Clint like a misplaced eye.

"What are you doing out here alone?" he asked as the girl drew closer.

"I escaped from *bandidos*," she explained breathlessly. "My name is Elena Jimenez and I—"

Suddenly, her wonderful eyes expanded in horror. Too late, Clint realized he'd turned his back on Pedro Castro. He caught a glimpse of a blur as the *bandido* launched himself from the saddle of his mustang.

Castro's bulky, muscular body crashed into the Gunsmith and both men toppled from Duke's back. Clint hit the ground hard with the bandit on top of him. His breath spewed from his lungs and for a moment he was too dazed to prevent Castro from plucking the Colt revolver from its holster.

Clint's right fist smashed into Castro's face before the bandit could use the gun. Castro's head recoiled from the punch and Clint quickly chopped the bottom of his fist into the man's bound wrists, knocking the Colt out of his hands.

Castro suddenly raised his doubled fists overhead and swung them at Clint's face. The Gunsmith jerked his head aside and the bandit's hands slammed into the ground next to Clint's ear. Clint's left fist whipped into Castro's jaw. The bandit's head turned sharply and Clint hit him again, driving his knuckles into Castro's right temple. The bandit sagged and most of his weight shifted from Clint.

The Gunsmith slid out from under Castro. He wanted to avoid a wrestling match with the bandit which would have been to the advantage of the larger, heavier man. Clint rolled away from his opponent and quickly rose to his feet.

Castro had rolled in the opposite direction. The bandit rolled right next to Clint's discarded .45 Colt. With a shout of victory, Castro seized the gun and swung it toward the Gunsmith.

"Things are different now, *gringo!*" Castro declared as he climbed to one knee and aimed the pistol at Clint's chest. "*Adiós, bastardo!*"

Castro cocked the hammer.

SIXTEEN

Elena Jimenez stepped behind Pedro Castro, holding a rock as big as a cannonball. Before the bandit's finger could squeeze the trigger of the Colt, Elena raised the rock high and brought it down on Castro's head. The Gunsmith heard the ugly crunch of bone breaking and the slush of oozing brains. Castro fell on his face without even uttering a grunt, the cocked revolver still in his fists.

Clint rushed forward and retrieved his gun. He didn't bother to check Castro's pulse because the bandit no longer had one. The top of his skull had been split open. Brains and blood gushed from the ghastly crack. Clint watched Elena toss the rock aside. Her face was taut with tension and her fingers trembled slightly, but the girl's eyes revealed only satisfaction with her deed.

"I never killed a man before," she said in a monotone. The girl seemed too overwhelmed by conflicting emotions to feel upset by her actions.

"I'm sort of glad you did it," Clint confessed. "Thank you, Elena. You saved my life."

"*Sí, señor*," She nodded woodenly. "The *bandidos* who follow el Espectro are not really men, you know. I did not truly kill a man. These brutes have no souls. They deserve to die, no?"

"Can't argue with that, Elena," the Gunsmith replied. "I guess you won't be too unhappy to learn I killed two other bandits back in San José."

Her eyes widened in alarm. "San José! That is my village and I am trying to get back home. Now you tell me el Espectro waits there?"

"No, Elena," Clint assured her. "He was there, looking for you. He left three men behind in case you returned, but he and the rest of his band left."

"Did they harm anyone in my village?" Elena asked fearfully.

"No." Clint grinned. "In fact, your *padre* taught one of them a lesson in the risks of taking God's name in vain that struck the bandit where it hurts the most. Your people are safe for now."

"Except for those who are still held prisoner in el Espectro's camp," she said sadly.

"I'd hoped to help the captives," the Gunsmith sighed. "I had Castro with me to guide me to the bandits' lair. Now that he's dead, I'm right back where I started."

"That is not true, *señor*," Elena replied. "I can take you to el Espectro's camp, no?"

Clint stared at the girl. Her face was determined, those big, magnificent eyes revealing eagerness. "No," he told her. "Absolutely not."

"But, *señor* . . ."

"Call me Clint." He smiled. "Look, Elena, I don't need to tell you what these bandits are like. You know that better than anyone. I'm not going to ask you to lead me back to their hideout. . . ."

"You do not have to ask, Clint," she said. "I offered, no?"

"From what I've heard," Clint began, "you're the

first person ever to escape from el Espectro's clutches. Do you want to take the chance of falling into his hands again?"

"If I return to San José and el Espectro comes back," Elena said stubbornly, "what do you think he will do then? He would punish all the people of my village, Clint."

"Maybe you have a point," the Gunsmith had to admit. "But . . . well, you're a girl and I don't think you'd be wise to tangle with these bandits."

"Oh?" She smiled. "Didn't you just thank me for saving your life, Clint?"

"Er . . . yeah," he confessed.

"I killed that *bandido*." Elena jerked her head toward the corpse of Pedro Castro. "And I won't mind killing others of his kind. It is self-defense, no? El Espectro has been killing my people for years. He not only abducts us at will, he robs us of our food and water, and worse, he has taken what dignity we have left. That is why I must go with you, Clint. My people will never be free until el Espectro has been destroyed."

"Okay, you've convinced me." The Gunsmith sighed. "But I have to warn you, so far my guides haven't had very good luck."

"Perhaps our luck is about to change," she replied.

"I hope so," he remarked. "I sure hope so."

SEVENTEEN

Elena Jimenez, astride the bandit's mustang, rode beside the Gunsmith as they continued on the journey to el Espectro's headquarters. The girl's memory was very good and she was certain they'd reach the bandit lair by sundown.

"Sundown?" Clint raised his eyebrows. "That means el Espectro's camp must be less than twenty miels away."

"It may be less than that, Clint," Elena replied.

"That means el Espectro's headquarters is located only one day's ride from Fort Juarez," Clint realized. "Why the hell haven't the *rurales* found the Ghost and his men? The *bandidos* can't be that well hidden."

"Their camp did not seem well hidden to me," Elena commented. "But you will see for yourself when we get there."

"I can hardly wait," the Gunsmith muttered. "Since you're willing to take on el Espectro, I guess you don't believe in the stories that he has supernatural powers."

"I'm not certain," Elena answered grimly. "The Ghost has some sort of powers—although I can't say if they are supernatural abilities or an unusually strong influence on people. His men believe he is a *brujo*—a male witch. Many people are convinced el Espectro is an evil spirit, a living corpse commanded by *el Diablo*. All I can tell you is he is very evil and very dangerous."

"Yeah." Clint recalled his own encounter with el

Espectro. "He's sure a *bandido* of a different color."

"Why are you so determined to find el Espectro, Clint?" the girl asked.

The Gunsmith explained his mission to Elena. She nodded and said, "I saw the Anglo girl once. She is very beautiful, with yellow hair and fair skin. El Espectro prizes her greatly for he keeps her in his house away from the rest of the women captives."

So Marsha Woodland is still alive, Clint thought. *There's still a chance to rescue her from the bandits.*

"I do not believe the Anglo girl has been harmed," Elena continued. "Though I am certain she has been raped by the Ghost's men. . . . We—we all were, of course."

"I'm sorry, Elena," Clint said softly.

"It is done," she replied. "Nothing can change that. I can only pray that their devil seed does not grow inside me."

The Gunsmith wanted to say something to comfort the girl, but realized words would be useless. "I understand el Espectro abducted men as well. What does he do with them?"

"They are forced to work as slaves," Elena answered. "El Espectro is trying to turn his camp into a fortress so he has captives constructing buildings and adobe walls. The workers are poorly fed and they do not survive long under the harsh treatment of the *bandido* guards who make liberal use of whips and boots to enforce discipline."

"Jesus." Clint shook his head. "What does this el Espectro think he is? A Mexican Caligula?"

"Perhaps he believes what he tells his men," Elena replied. "That he is the bridge between Life and Death."

"Sounds like it's about time somebody severed his connection to the former," the Gunsmith said grimly.

EIGHTEEN

"We're very close now," Elena warned. She thrust a finger to the west. "If we ride another mile or so in that direction, sentries posted on the wall might see us."

"Do the bandits have telescopes?" Clint inquired.

"Telescopes?" The girl's brow wrinkled. "No, they don't."

"Well, I do," Clint declared as he swung down from Duke's back and opened a saddlebag to remove his Dolland—a collapsible pocket telescope favored by sailors.

The couple had arrived at a prairie which featured numerous rock formations as well as patches of mesquite, sagebrush, and some cottonwood trees. This was another indication that they were approaching the hideout because the vegetation in such an arid region suggested an underground stream, and Elena had told Clint the bandits had a well in their camp.

Clint ground-hobbled the mustang, but left Duke untied because he knew the big gelding wouldn't wander off. The Gunsmith and Elena scaled a tall butte with a relatively flat summit. From the elevated position, Clint saw a cluster of adobe structures surrounded by a partially built wall which formed a horseshoe shape around the buildings. From a distance, it resembled the ruins of an ancient city. Clint opened his

Dolland and raised it to his eye.

El Espectro's camp was everything Elena had described—and worse. The wall was far from complete, but bandits stood sentry on it. The guards gazed down at the campsite, rifles held loosely in their hands. They were watching an assortment of scrawny *peónes* hauling adobe bricks and mortar to the wall. Other bandits supervised the slaves in the construction of the barricade.

The structures within the camp varied. Several tents surrounded a large *hacienda*. The Moorish-style great house would have been a fitting home for a wealthy rancher or the owner of a coffee plantation. Whatever else one might say about el Espectro, he had good taste.

There was also a large tent located at the south wall of the camp. A fat bandit, seated at a military field desk, wearily guarded a pile of guns and knives stacked beside his desk. At the west wall stood an adobe prison with a door made of iron bars.

"Elena," Clint urged, handing her the Dolland, "look down at the camp and identify everything for me."

"The *hacienda* is el Espectro's house," she replied, gazing through the lens. "He and his *tenientes* are there as well as the Woodland girl you came here to rescue."

"What about the tents?"

"The smaller ones are for the rank-and-file bandits. The tents comprise a bivouac area for them," the girl explained.

"Jesus," Clint whispered. "Then there must be almost fifty men in el Espectro's gang."

"I did not count them, but I would say that number is about right."

"I've got to quit getting myself into this kind of situation," the Gunsmith muttered. "Okay, Elena. What's in the big tent? The one with the fella stationed at the table beside the pile of weapons?"

"That is where the women prisoners are held," she replied bitterly. "I know that tent well. The *bandidos* who aren't carrying out assigned duties are allowed to enter the tent and force themselves on the women. They consider it to be a *casa de las putas*—a whorehouse—but the girls inside do not act willingly. . . ."

"I understand, Elena," Clint assured her. "Now, why is that guy at the desk with all those guns?"

"The men who enter the tent are required to leave their weapons outside," Elena answered. "El Espectro gave this order because he doesn't want the women to get an opportunity to take a gun or knife away from a drunken *bandido*."

"Makes sense," Clint mused. "Okay, the adobe jailhouse is obviously where they keep the male prisoners. What about the sentries on the wall? They seem to be guarding the slave laborers. They don't seem to be watching for anyone approaching the camp from the outside."

"*Sí!*" Elena agreed. "You are right, Clint! I recall now, the guards are not posted on the wall after dark when the prisoners are locked in their cells."

"So, el Espectro isn't worried that anyone will locate his camp and pull his half-built fortress down around his lily-white ears." The Gunsmith smiled coldly. "His overconfidence has left a nice big gap in his security. Now, all we have to do is find a way to take advantage of it."

NINETEEN

Clint Adams checked his weapons as the orange sun sank into the western sky. Besides his Springfield carbine and modified double-action .45 revolver, Clint had added another gun to his arsenal—a .22-caliber New Line Colt which had previously been in his saddlebag. He often carried the diminutive pistol under his shirt, tucked in his belt as a belly gun. It had saved his life more than once and he figured it wouldn't hurt to take all the firepower he could carry when they hit el Espectro's camp.

The plan he and Elena had devised was risky, but there wasn't any safe, logical or sane way for two people to attack an enemy stronghold. The scheme would depend on stealth and cunning more than bullets—in fact, any shooting would mean they were both as good as dead. Not even the Gunsmith could take on fifty gunmen in an open battle, but if their plan went sour, Clint intended to take as many *bandidos* as possible with him to the grave.

"Clint?" Elena's voice called gently as she approached, carrying a blanket in her arms. "We may both die tonight, no?"

"Honey"—he sighed—"there aren't any sure things in this world. You might roll out of bed and break your neck. You can choke to death on a chicken-bone or get struck by lightning when you're heading home from church. I'm not a prophet and I wouldn't want to be. I can't tell you if we'll see the sunrise or not. All I know is we've both decided to hit el Espectro and we've figured out a plan that seems to have a good chance of success. We can't do more than that, Elena.''

"I know," she declared as she laid the blanket on the ground beside him. "I can accept death, but I do not want to die before I—before I know . . ."

Clint saw the embarrassment in her lovely young face. Then he glanced at the blanket. He knew what she meant. The girl had been raised to consider sex as an intimate, beautiful relationship between a man and a woman—probably reserved only for husband and wife. Yet, she hadn't known the gentleness and warmth of making love. She'd been introduced instead to the vicious, perverse act of rape. She'd been beaten and ravaged by animals. Her virginity had not been given away by choice, but ripped from her by the barbarians in el Espectro's gang.

"Elena," he said gently, "all that you were taught in the past—that making love is a beautiful experience, that it can fulfill and satisfy the body and spirit—it is all true."

"I—I don't know. . . ."

"Don't say anything," he urged. "Just sit down here beside me and we'll share ourselves willingly— the way a man and a woman are meant to."

She sank to her knees on the blanket. Clint cupped her face in his hands and gazed into Elena's big, beautiful eyes. They were so dark and deep and soft, filled with warmth and passion. He saw no fear or apprehension in them. Clint pressed his lips against her wide, luscious mouth. She responded eagerly, returning his kiss with uninhibited enthusiasm.

Her lips were wonderful, soft and moist. Clint probed inside her mouth with his tongue. Elena responded by embracing his neck and pulling him closer. Their hands soon explored each other's body as the fires of desire were stirred by increased passion. Clint felt the girl's nipples strain against the fabric of her tattered dress as he caressed her breasts. She groaned with pleasure and slowly slid her hands across his shoulders and back.

The Gunsmith dropped a hand to her skirt and gradually hiked up her dress. His manhood swelled at the sight of her shapely, naked legs and the touch of her warm, smooth flesh. Clint stroked her thighs, slowly working his hand higher. Elena responded by caressing his crotch. She gasped when she felt his hardened member.

"Oh, *sí!*" the girl crooned. "*Sí!*"

Clint hastily removed his clothing, placing his gunbelt within arm's reach. It was crazy to make love like this, with an enemy stronghold less than two miles away. A group of el Espectro's bandits might happen along at any moment.

Yet, it would have been insane to ignore the needs of a beautiful, sensitive young girl and to deny himself the ecstasy of her body. In a few hours there would be killing and Clint and Elena might well be dead. Now, however, there was time for love and to allow the opportunity to slip by them would have been the greatest lunacy of all.

Elena removed her dress, revealing her gorgeous brown body in the glory of its nakedness. The girl examined Clint with frank admiration as she stroked his bare flesh and allowed him to reply with his own skillful, gentle touch.

Their coupling was gradual. Clint took his time, aware that Elena needed to feel the warmth and tenderness of making love. She needed to know that sex was not always brutal and selfish. He entered her slowly and worked his hips to gently ease his throbbing organ deeper.

Although his desire raged within his loins and he wanted to thrust harder, Clint held back his own yearning until Elena began to wiggle and buck beneath him. Then he pumped his manhood faster and deeper inside her. Elena stifled a cry of joy and clung to her lover.

They convulsed and groaned, resisting the urge to shout their pleasures in the night. Then Elena's marvelous legs wrapped around Clint's hips, drawing him closer as she trembled in the throes of an orgasm. Clint had also reached the zenith. He exploded his seed into her hot, damp chamber of love.

"It *is* true, Clint," Elena whispered. "*Gracias a Dios!* It is true."

TWENTY

The Gunsmith and Elena approached the bandit camp from the south side. The night sky was illuminated by a half moon and a sprinkling of stars. Clint and the girl favored the darkest shadows available as they surreptitiously crept toward el Espectro's headquarters.

The *bandido* hideout was pretty active that night—which suited the Gunsmith. With plenty of men milling about the camp, the bandits wouldn't be apt to pay much attention to another figure dressed in a sombrero and serape. Drunken voices sang Spanish ballads and a handful of el Espectro's men staggered from tent to tent. Some paused to relieve themselves on the ground. One man pissed on his own boots without realizing it. Male laughter and occasional female screams came from the large tent, still guarded by the fat bandit at the field desk. The slaves, however, had been returned to jail and the sentries who had formerly been positioned on the wall were no longer on duty.

Stunned by el Espectro's lack of security for his camp, Clint and Elena simply climbed over the incomplete wall and entered the stronghold. Still dressed in the hat and poncho Father Rameriz had given him in San José, Clint knew he could pass for a rather tall Mexican providing no one got close enough to notice his skin was merely tanned by the sun or discovered he spoke only a smattering of Spanish. Hoping his disguise would work well enough in the dark, Clint pretended to be drunk and staggered toward the large tent.

"*Buenas noches, amigo,*" he greeted the beefy bandit at the desk.

"*Sí, sí,*" the fat man replied in a weary voice.

He yawned as he watched Clint place his Springfield carbine on the stack of weapons. Suddenly, the sentry's eyes widened when he noticed the Gunsmith's face was not familiar to him.

"*Uno momento!*" the bandit snapped. "*Quién es?*"

"*Qué?*" Clint muttered in a slurred voice. "*Quién soy yo?*"

"*Sí!*" the guard insisted, his hand reaching for a revolver thrust in his belt.

Elena had taken advantage of the distraction created by the brief conversation between Clint and the sentry. Moving quickly and silently on bare feet, the girl crept up behind the unsuspecting *bandido* and slammed the hard, knotty end of a cottonwood club down on the man's skull. The sentry groaned and fell face first on the desk.

Clint glanced about, ready to reach for the .45 hidden beneath his poncho. However, no one had seen Elena slug the bandit. The camp appeared to be deserted and the only sounds were the grunting noises of crude sex within the large tent, which Elena and Clint now entered together.

Inside, the tent was almost pitch black, the only source of light being holes in the canvas that allowed some moonlight to enter from above. Clint and Elena let their eyes adjust to the darkness. The Gunsmith recalled what Elena had told him about the design of the "women's prison." The tent was divided into five "rooms"—actually stalls with only partitions of canvas to separate the women, who each had a cot, water, one dress, and nothing else.

The *bandidos* would enter the tent and help themselves to any woman they wanted, providing someone else wasn't already occupied with her. Of course, the men were required to leave their weapons outside. This included such items as tequila bottles, forks or even spoons which could be improvised as weapons by a desperate, vengeful woman against a drunken, lustful man. Trying to resist or fight bare-handed was hopeless and would only earn the woman a vicious beating before being raped by the *bandidos*.

Clint saw five stalls. One, formerly Elena's, was currently empty. Each of the other four contained a woman and a *bandido* "customer." The Gunsmith could only guess how difficult it was for Elena to return to the tent. How much abuse, humiliation and pain had she suffered within that canvas hellhole? The girl had incredible courage to step across the threshold once again to try to rescue the others still held captive by el Espectro.

They moved to the nearest stall. Inside a young woman lay on a cot, staring up at the canvas ceiling. The bandit lying next to her snored loudly. Clint took the cudgel from Elena.

"*Calla te, Maria,*" Elena whispered to the other woman.

The girl stared at them. "Elena?" she whispered in return.

"*Sí,*" Elena confirmed.

While Elena whispered more information to the other woman, Clint made certain the bandit continued to sleep for quite a while. He swung the club with all his might and hit the sleeping *bandido* twice in the forehead. Bone crunched and a half-grunt, half-sigh escaped from the man's lips. He would never wake again.

"*Gracias, señor,*" a feminine voice said near Clint's ear.

Then a wide, soft mouth pressed against his lips. The kiss was brief, but sweet and filled with fire. The Gunsmith was certain it was Maria, not Elena, who had delivered the kiss.

"I've explained everything. . . ." Elena whispered, but Clint placed a finger to her lips to silence the girl.

While Maria pulled on a dress, Clint and Elena moved to the next stall. A *bandido* was on top of a girl. He grunted and giggled as he pumped himself between her splayed legs. The girl lay on her back stiffly, unwillingly submitting to the man's action, yet she dared not resist, well aware of the terrible price she'd have to pay for rebellion.

Clint found the bandit's head and smashed the club into it. The man groaned and slumped unconscious on the girl. The Gunsmith quickly put a hand over her mouth before she could cry out in alarm. Elena knelt by the cot and whispered to the girl, who relaxed and nodded to express her understanding of the situation.

The Gunsmith turned and prepared to leave the stall. The figure of a man blocked his path. The bandit said something that sounded like a question to Clint.

"*Tequila!*" The Gunsmith laughed as he staggered toward the figure. "*Tequila!*"

The other man chuckled in response. Then Clint swung a roundhouse right and rapped the club against the side of the man's jaw. Before the bandit could fall, Clint caught him by the shirt front with his left hand and rammed the end of the cudgel into the fellow's midsection. The *bandido* doubled up with a rasping cough and Clint delivered another blow to the base of his skull.

"*Qué la chigada!*" a masculine voice exclaimed.

Clint turned to see a shadow rushing toward him. He tried to raise the club, but the bandit crashed into him and knocked the weapon from the Gunsmith's grasp. Both men lost their balance and fell against a partition. Canvas ripped and they toppled on a cot, landing on one of the *bandidos* Clint had previously clubbed into unconsciousness . . . or death.

A girl screamed and one of the other women slapped her and told her to shut up. Clint wrestled with his opponent until he managed to ram a knee into the man's groin. He followed with a right cross to the bandit's jaw. The man sagged. Clint's fist hit him behind the ear. The *bandido* fell to the ground. The Gunsmith knelt on his dazed adversary and punched him twice more in the face to be certain he'd stay down.

Clint rose and hurried to the entrance, drawing his Colt .45 revolver as he ran. However, his concern proved needless. The bandits were accustomed to the sounds of occasional brawls in the women's tent and no one seemed alarmed.

Two figures clad in long underwear and sombreros stood by one of the bivouac tents, staring back at Clint Adams. One of them shouted something at Clint which the Gunsmith didn't understand, but the tone of the man's voice sounded as if he had made a joke. Clint holstered his Colt and raised his arms and shoulders in an exaggerated shrug. The two men laughed in reply. The Gunsmith slipped back inside the tent.

"What do we do now?" Elena asked.

"I'm going to haul our fat friend in here," Clint replied, referring to the unconscious sentry at the field desk. "We're lucky nobody noticed him slumped over napping."

"Won't they notice he's missing?" Elena inquired.

"I'll take his place. Hopefully no one will wander over here again tonight."

He stepped outside and propped up the sentry. The man's eyes stared at him without comprehension and Clint realized the fellow wasn't just unconscious after all. *Elena sure knows how to hit,* he thought.

Clint pretended to talk to the dead man until he was certain none of the bandits was watching. Then he dragged the corpse into the tent. Elena and Maria were waiting for him and helped carry the man inside.

"Okay," Clint began, "you girls wait here until I tell you we're ready to carry out the rest of our plan. Find that club and keep an eye on the bandits. If any of them seems to be about to regain consciousness . . ."

"Don't worry about that," Maria said in fluent, if rather cold English. "Just give me a knife. I'll make certain they'll never wake again, no?"

The Gunsmith stared at the woman. She was tall and sleek with jet black hair and a fiercely beautiful face with bright dark eyes and a ripe mouth. Yet, she clearly meant what she'd said.

"You plan to slit the throats of unarmed, unconscious men?" he asked.

"If we could spare the time and didn't have to worry about them screaming in the night," Maria replied,

"I'd poke out their eyes and cut off their *cojones* before I killed them."

Clint frowned. "Well, I guess you ladies have suffered enough at the hands of these bastards. Maybe you deserve a little revenge." He shrugged. "Killing these bandits is sort of like shooting mad dogs anyway."

"Not quite," Maria smiled. "I would not *enjoy* killing a mad dog."

TWENTY-ONE

Clint Adams sat behind the field desk at the mouth of the tent. He gazed over the camp, noting a sleepy-eyed sentry positioned at the jail which contained the male prisoners. No one else seemed to remain outside their quarters.

He glanced over the weapons pile. The collection consisted of four gunbelts and an assortment of Bowie knives, daggers and two rifles, including his Springfield carbine. Clint hesitated for a moment before he picked up one of the Bowies and tossed the knife into the tent for Maria.

The Gunsmith waited almost half an hour to be certain none of the bandits was still awake. Then he rose from his chair and calmly strolled toward the sentry posted by the jailhouse. The bandit guard saw him approach and rose from his stool. He left a Greener shotgun propped against an adobe wall as he stepped forward to meet the Gunsmith.

"Surprise!" Clint rasped, suddenly drawing his Colt and pointing the muzzle at the bandit's face.

The man raised his arms and muttered either a prayer or a curse under his breath. His eyes were locked on Clint's gun so he didn't see the Gunsmith's leg slash out, although he certainly felt the nerve-blasting agony of the kick to his genitals. The bandit groaned, folded and fell to his knees. Clint slammed the butt of his revolver into the base of the fellow's neck. Vertebrae cracked and the man collapsed with a broken neck.

Clint waved at the women's tent. Elena, Maria and the other three girls emerged. All but one grabbed guns from the weapon pile before rushing forward to join the Gunsmith. Clint knelt beside the sentry and checked for a pulse. The man was dead. Clint frisked him for a key to the jailhouse. He wasn't surprised when he didn't find one. El Espectro's security of his prisoners was better than his protection for the camp itself.

"Tell the prisoners to be quiet," Clint said to the women. "They'll be free in a few minutes, but we can't have any noise or we'll be slaughtered."

"Did you find the key to their cell?" Elena asked.

"No," he replied as he stripped the dead man of his weapons.

"Then how will you free the prisoners?" she inquired.

"I'll manage," Clint assured her.

"Our hero has done pretty well so far," Maria declared with a grin. "I trust you, Clint."

"Sure hope I can live up to your confidence in me, ma'am," he grinned in reply.

Elena relayed Clint's message to the male prisoners. They clung to the bars of the jailhouse door, their faces aglow with expectation, yet they managed to remain silent—perhaps because the women had done so well at being quiet thus far.

Clint Adams knelt by the door and examined the lock. From what he could see by the moonlight, it appeared to be pretty standard—a regular two-tumbler model. From his back pocket he removed a small package wrapped in oilcloth.

Opening it, he selected two tools generally used for his gunsmithing work. The slim metal cartridge probe was designed to pry warped shell casings from a gun breech or barrel and to remove broken firing pins or springs. The other device was a slender hacksaw blade used for modifying guns that required delicate metal cutting.

He inserted the saw blade into the lock, allowing the teeth of the flexible metal to search for the tumblers inside. When they caught on the metal within, he slid the probe in and slowly worked both tools. Lockpicking wasn't one of Clint's greatest talents, but thirty seconds later, he heard the lock click and the door was open.

The *peónes* had to suppress a desire to cheer out loud and more than one couldn't resist a soft "Oooh!" in admiration of Clint's success. The Gunsmith put his tools away and turned to Elena.

"Okay, Elena," he began, "I want you to lead everybody out of here. Take the weapons with you, but don't use them unless you have to. Leave the same way we got in and take everybody to the rocks where we left Duke and the other horse."

"But what will you do?" she inquired, concern etched on her lovely face.

"I've still got a little unfinished business to take care of," Clint replied. "You folks wait for me at the rocks. If I'm not there in two hours—then you'll just have to go on without me."

"Clint . . ." Elena and Maria began at the same time.

"Hey, don't gang up on me." He grinned. "I thought you trusted me. Get going."

Reluctantly, the girls nodded in agreement. Maria

had picked up Clint's Springfield from the weapon pile. She offered the carbine to him. Clint shook his head.

"You keep it," he said. "You can give it back to me later."

Or else I won't need it anyway, the Gunsmith thought.

TWENTY-TWO

The *peónes* shuffled out of the camp and disappeared over the half-built wall at the south side of the fortress. Clint dragged the dead sentry into the jail and closed the door before he headed for the *hacienda*—alone.

The Gunsmith mounted the steps of the main house and drew his pistol. With his left hand, he turned the doorknob. Clint was surprised and almost disappointed to find the door unlocked. He'd done so well picking the lock at the jail, he'd almost have welcomed a chance to test his ability again. He'd also know if his hands were as steady as they should be.

Clint opened the door and entered a spacious hallway. To his surprise and relief, there were no guards stationed in the corridor. In fact, the hall was totally bare, consisting of nothing but whitewashed walls and a solid adobe floor. The Gunsmith had half expected to find carpets and oil paintings in the house.

The hell with it, he told himself. *The only riddle I have to solve is where is Marsha Woodland? After I've found the girl, I have to get her and myself out of here before the Mexican boogey man or his gang find out what happened.*

Clint moved through the hallway, his revolver held ready. The antiseptic appearance of the corridor disturbed him for a reason he could only guess. Perhaps it reminded him of the hospitals and insane asylums back East . . . or maybe the naked white adobe seemed too much like the interior of a mausoleum.

The Gunsmith discovered several doors. He touched the panel of one and strained his eyes to try to confirm what his fingers told him. *Jesus*, Clint thought. *This is made of redwood from the California forest! How the hell did el Espectro get something like this in the middle of a Sonora desert?*

Then Clint noticed a pale strip of yellow light which extended from the bottom of one of the doors. The Gunsmith immediately moved to the door and grabbed its knob. Gently, he turned it and eased the door open, poking the muzzle of his Colt through the space.

The room was fully furnished with handsome leather-backed chairs and a walnut desk as well as a liquor cabinet and end tables and a large bookcase. It had all the trimmings of a wealthy man's office, complete with wallpaper, carpet and an oil painting hung behind the desk—a painting of a skeleton clad in a black shroud with a scythe held in its bony hands.

Yet, the office itself didn't startle the Gunsmith as much as discovering the apparition seated in an armchair with a book in one hand and a balloon glass of brandy in the other. The creature strongly resembled the portrait of the Grim Reaper with its pale features and knobby long fingers. El Espectro looked up at Clint Adams, his gaunt face impassive and his gaze as cold and steady as that of a rattlesnake.

"It is impolite to enter a room without knocking," the Ghost said in a soft voice that contained a slight reptilian hiss. "But, then, it is rude to point a gun at your host as well."

Clint entered the room and eased the door shut. El Espectro was the most incredible being the Gunsmith had ever encountered. The bandit chief still wore his black cowl, but the hood was down, revealing snow white hair, the same color as his skin. El Espectro wasn't wearing his glasses with the smoked lenses. His eyes were an unnatural shade of light red, the color of pale blood. The Ghost seemed calm as he placed his book on an end table.

"You are a *norteamericano*, aren't you?" el Espectro inquired in impeccable English. He sounded like a Harvard graduate. "If you don't understand me, I also speak French, Italian and, of course, Spanish."

"I understand you, fella," Clint assured him, aiming the gun at el Espectro's head. "Do you understand that I'll kill you if you try anything?"

"Oh, yes." The Ghost smiled. "I'm certain you would try, Mr. . . .?"

"Adams. Clint Adams."

"Adams?" El Espectro took a thoughtful sip of brandy. "I've heard that name before. . . .ah! You're the one they call the Gunsmith, correct?"

"That's right," Clint admitted.

"Life can truly be amazing," the Ghost mused. "You and I are both very famous men. We've both acquired reputations associated with Death. Here we meet, in an obscure desert called the Devil's Belly. Quite remarkable, isn't it?"

"Never know who you'll come across in a new place," Clint agreed. "How come you're reading a book with the lamplight turned so low?"

"My affliction makes me a bit nearsighted and terribly sensitive to light," el Espectro replied.

"That's why you wear those smoked glasses, eh?"

"Indeed." The Ghost nodded, "In fact, I try to avoid going anywhere in the daylight unless it is necessary. One of the drawbacks I've had to learn to cope with."

"Yeah," the Gunsmith commented, "I guess life isn't easy for an albino bandit."

"Ah! So you realize I'm an albino," el Espectro declared. "But, of course, you're an educated man. Most people think I'm an evil spirit. Rather amusing, isn't it?"

"You do your best to live up to their expectations," Clint told him.

"I suppose that's true." The Ghost shrugged. "But, then, I've got to try harder than most to be successful, and playing a personification of Death rather suits me.

"Do you know what an albino is, Mr. Adams?" el Espectro continued, swallowing the last of his brandy. "It is a freak of nature which has a flaw in the pigmentation of its skin, hair, even its eyes. Any kind of animal can give birth to such a freak—cattle, fish, spiders; there are even albino crows. However, albinos are very rare, and in most cases they do quite poorly since they have weak eyesight and they tend to be physically weak and sickly."

"Sorry," Clint snorted. "I didn't bring my violin."

"No need to feel any sympathy for me." The albino laughed. "You see, when I was very young, I decided to concentrate on improving myself in every possible way to cheat nature of its attempt to make me a failure in life. As a child, I was often sick and I was shunned by my peers, yet I accepted this and strived to work harder. I studied and exerted myself in school and later in college. I was still a freak, but I was also a brilliant student with a talent for management and organization."

"So why are you leading a bunch of ragtag bandits if you're so smart?" Clint asked.

"Well, the world of business has its snobs." El Espectro sighed. "And they didn't want me to be part of it. After all, why hire a freak if you don't have to? Albinos belong in a sideshow with the dwarfs, pinheads, and the dog-faced boy, right? Not *this* albino, Mr. Adams. I took advantage of my appearance and, yes, I used the superstitious nature of the Mexican *peónes*. Why not? Do you know what it's like to be brilliant and resourceful yet see other less qualified 'normal' men receive jobs and promotions instead? My past failures and my present success all revolve around the fact I am an albino."

"So you had some hard knocks and you're making innocent people suffer because of it." The Gunsmith shook his head. "I've met your kind before, fella. They weren't albinos, but their excuse for violence and destruction was always the same. You'll get no pity from me, Mr. Ghost. All you can expect is a bullet if you don't do exactly as I say."

"Then you're finally going to explain the reason for your uninvited visit." The bandit laughed. "You must have a very good reason. Creeping into my camp, surrounded by my men, taking so many chances . . . for what?"

"I've come for Marsha Woodland," Clint said in a hard, flat voice.

"Ah!" The albino nodded. "So the congressman decided not to pay the ransom. Instead he chose to hire the Gunsmith. How melodramatic of him and how foolish of *you* to accept the task."

"Is that a fact?" Clint smiled. "Looks like I've got the drop on you, Mr. Ghost."

"True," the albino admitted. "But if you fire that

gun, the shots will attract my men. Even you can't fight your way through more than forty armed *bandidos*, Mr. Adams"

"Perhaps not," Clint agreed. "But you'll be dead anyway, so you really won't get much satisfaction about that. Unless they have a telegraph office in Hell, you might not even get to know about it."

"You really are amusing, Mr. Adams," el Espectro stated as he rose from his chair. "Very well. I'll take you to the damsel in distress . . . not that you'll live to rescue her."

TWENTY-THREE

El Espectro inserted a hand under his black cloak. Clint Adams cocked the hammer of his Colt revolver. "Easy, fella," the Gunsmith warned. "Even if you have a holdout gun, we'll both die together if you shoot me."

"I'm not that rash, Mr. Adams," the albino told him as he extracted a ring of keys from a pocket.

"You're making a good start at staying alive, Mr. Ghost," Clint said. "How many men do you have in this house?"

"Eight," el Espectro replied. "But no one patrols the building if that's what you're concerned about. Nor is there a guard posted at Miss Woodland's door."

"That's a bit careless, isn't it?"

"Not really," the albino replied. "Even if she escaped from her room, where would she run to in the middle of the desert?"

"What did you plan to do with her after you got your five thousand dollars from Woodland?"

"A moot point since her father sent you instead of the ransom." The Ghost shrugged. "Oh, I've got a deal arranged with a man to sell her to a brothel in Guatemala. The slavers were delighted when they learned I had a blonde Anglo for them. They're going to pay me one thousand dollars for the girl. Supply and demand, you know. Now, do you have any other immaterial questions?''

"How did you know Woodland and his daughter would be at Fred Barsa's ranch the day you abducted the girl?" Clint asked.

"I've heard you're a rather good detective, Mr. Adams," the albino replied. "What's your guess?"

"I figure somebody on Barsa's staff must have told you about it and then you watched the ranch from a safe distance until the time was right before you moved in."

"Excellent!" El Espectro smiled. "You're right, of course. The contact, by the way, was the housekeeper. We killed the woman to make certain she didn't reveal anything to Woodland or Barsa. She had already betrayed her employer's trust, so we couldn't take the chance she'd do the same to us."

"And, of course, you didn't have to pay her then," Clint said grimly.

"Not much sense in paying a corpse, is there?"

"Marsha Woodland had better be alive, fella," the Gunsmith warned. "Now, you take me to her and you'd better do exactly as I tell you—unless you're eager to meet up with your hero the Grim Reaper."

"Shall we go, Mr. Adams?" El Espectro smiled thinly.

The albino guided Clint through the corridors. The Gunsmith followed his evil host, keeping the .45 trained on el Espectro's back. Although the albino continued to obey Clint and offered no resistance, he still seemed too calm and self-assured for the circumstances. It was unnatural for any man to be so nonchalant when faced with the likelihood of his own death. The Gunsmith sensed something was wrong, but he couldn't act until he had some idea what it was.

"Here is the girl's room," el Espectro announced as he stopped in front of another redwood door and grabbed its brass knob.

"Open it," Clint ordered.

"Of course, my *norteamericano pistolero* friend," the Ghost remarked, raising his voice slightly.

Instantly, Clint realized what el Espectro had done. He'd led the Gunsmith to a room and told whoever waited behind that door what to expect—an Anglo gunfighter.

The door wasn't locked and the albino suddenly turned the knob and shoved it open. Clint held his fire a moment too long and el Espectro dove into the room. Then a fierce-faced figure with a drooping mustache appeared within the room with a cut-down Henry carbine in his fists. Clint didn't hesitate again. He shot the man through the heart before the bandit could open fire.

Without warning, white hands reached from inside the room and seized the Gunsmith. One hand closed around Clint's wrist behind the gun while the other caught him by the throat. El Espectro's face, a death mask in white marble, materialized before the Gunsmith's eyes. The albino's hands were incredibly powerful for such a thin man. Already the chokehold at Clint's throat was cutting off his air and the grip on his wrist had effectively forced his gun toward the ceiling.

El Espectro suddenly kicked one of Clint's feet out from under him and both men fell to the floor. The albino landed on top, a bent knee hitting Clint in the diaphragm. The Gunsmith struggled, but el Espectro rapped the back of his head against the floor to daze Clint.

The albino's grip on Clint's wrist still kept his gun immobile and he shifted a knee to pin the Gunsmith's left arm as well. The hand at Clint's throat squeezed harder. Clint saw el Espectro smile with satisfaction as he throttled his victim. Spots of light burst in front of Clint's eyes and he felt the .45 Colt slip from his fingers.

"I am sure you were warned, Mr. Adams," a voice echoed in the corridor. "El Espectro *is* Death. . . ."

The Gunsmith's strength vanished and he could no longer fight the ghostly figure that held him helpless on the floor while it strangled him. A black veil descended over his consciousness and he sank into oblivion. . . .

TWENTY-FOUR

"Mr. Adams!"

The sound roared from a deep, endless tunnel somewhere in the void. Clint wished the voice would go away. *Hell, you're supposed to rest in peace after you've been strangled to death.*

"Adams!"

Go to hell, Clint thought.

Something cold and wet splashed over the Gunsmith and he was abruptly yanked into consciousness. His eyes opened slowly to see a hazy white bulb. He blinked and the mist vanished. El Espectro's pale face, now wearing the dark glasses, stared back at him.

"I hope I didn't choke you too hard, Adams," the albino declared in a hard voice as he held a ladle to the Gunsmith's mouth. "You've got some explaining to do."

Clint eagerly drank. The water massaged his dry throat, which was still bruised and sore from his near strangulation. As his head cleared, the Gunsmith became aware of a dull ache in his arms. They were extended overhead and held fast by manacles. Clint was shackled to a T-shaped wooden frame. He realized it was a whipping post, the type used by the Army to administer corporal punishment. Leg irons secured his ankles to the ground.

He'd been stripped to the waist; of course, his New Line Colt hideout gun had been discovered and confiscated. Clint's boots had also been taken and his pockets had been turned inside out. He realized he was outside even before he saw the pale, pink dawn sky and the soft white sun of early morning.

Clint glanced about and recognized the various buildings of the bandit camp. He also saw more than thirty brutal-faced *bandidos*—and every one of them looked like he'd find great pleasure in skinning the Gunsmith alive with a rusty knife.

"Talk, Adams!" el Espectro ordered sharply. All his sophisticated charm was gone. The bandit leader was angry and he didn't bother to hide his emotions now. "I didn't crush your larynx, did I?"

The Gunsmith didn't reply. He tried to clear his mind.

"My strength caught you off guard, didn't it, Adams?" the albino continued. "I told you I had to work harder. One of the things I've done is to exercise my fingers every day to develop a powerful grip. I could have killed you, but I want you to talk first."

Clint remained silent.

"Of course, if you can't talk"—the Ghost shrugged—"we may as well kill you now. . . ."

"Go haunt a house, you bastard," the Gunsmith rasped hoarsely.

"That's better." El Espectro smiled. "Things will go better for you if you cooperate."

He barked a sentence in Spanish and two *bandidos* dragged a third figure over to Clint Adams. The Gunsmith stared at their prisoner. Marsha Woodland proved to be just as beautiful as the stories about her had claimed.

The girl appeared to be in her late teens or early twenties. She was five six or so and the tattered remnants of the blue gingham dress that clung to her body did not conceal a magnificent full bosom, wide hips and long tapered legs. Her hair was long and blonde. It needed to be washed and brushed, yet some of the luster still remained. Even the faded purple bruises on her cheeks did not detract from the loveliness of her face as her sky blue eyes stared back at the Gunsmith.

"Miss Woodland," el Espectro began, "meet Mr. Clint Adams, who was sent by your father to rescue you. He didn't do a very good job, but it was a nice thought, eh?"

The *bandido* chief chuckled softly. Then, without warning, he smashed the back of his hand into the Gunsmith's face. Clint's head rolled sharply from the blow and he felt himself swim toward unconsciousness once more. El Espectro seized him by the hair and jerked his face closer.

"You killed seven of my men, Adams!" the albino hissed. "You liberated my *peón* slaves and the women who entertained my men on lonely cold nights. My men are angry with you, Adams. So am I."

"Hey"—Clint forced a smile—"let's not cry over spilt milk. . . ."

The remark earned him another backhand swat in the mouth. Clint nearly blacked out. He tasted blood and his vision blurred for a moment.

"You are going to talk, Adams," el Espectro said fiercely. "You're going to tell us where our prisoners went and who helped you find my camp. Oh, yes. You will talk."

Clint turned his head toward Marsha Woodland. "I'm sorry I let you down, ma'am," he said gently.

"But don't figure all the poker chips have been cashed in. The game's not over yet."

The albino ordered his men to take Marsha away. She craned her neck to watch Clint as they dragged her back to the *hacienda*. The girl's eyes pleaded with him for help. *Shit*, the Gunsmith thought. *I'm chained to a goddamn whipping post. How the hell am I going to help anyone—including myself?*

"You astonish me, Adams." El Espectro shook his head. "If you honestly think you can escape now, you are truly insane."

"You ought to be an authority on that subject, whitey," Clint replied.

The gunsmith expected another slap, but el Espectro ignored the barb. "You're going to die, Adams," he said. "It can be quick by a bullet in the head, or it can be slow. Very slow. Do you know how the Yaqui Indians kill their victims, Adams?"

Clint wasn't likely to forget the two mutilated corpses he'd encountered on the trail. A shudder traveled along his spine.

"The Yaqui are experts at torture," the albino continued. "And quite a few of my men are Yaqui or half-breeds with Yaqui blood. That's why I don't have to worry about the Indians. A lot of their relatives work for me. Even my men who are not part Yaqui have acquired a good practical knowledge of the arts of torture. They know how to slice off eyelids to let your eyes roast in the sun. They know how to skin a man alive or cut off the tip of his penis and then cauterize it to keep him from bleeding to death."

"You guys must throw some pretty wild parties," Clint commented, trying to sound more brave than he felt.

"Make it easier on yourself, Adams." The Ghost lowered his face to stare at Clint. "Where are the fugitives?"

"I'm not really sure," the Gunsmith answered. "But let me loose and I'll help you look for them."

Suddenly, el Espectro's hand snaked forward and clawed into Clint's crotch. Steel talons gripped into his genitals. The Gunsmith gasped and convulsed in agony, but the chains held him fast. The albino squeezed harder and Clint almost screamed in response.

"I'll burst your testicles like a *piñata* unless you talk!" el Espectro snarled.

Then he released the Gunsmith. Clint gasped, drawing air into his lungs as the pain slowly began to subside. Through tear-blurred eyes, he saw el Espectro turn to face five men on horseback who had ridden into the bandit camp.

Clint blinked to clear his vision and saw the uniformed figures of the newcomers. He blinked again, unable to be certain what he saw was real. The riders were still there, clad in tan uniforms, black riding boots and ornate badges pinned to the crowns of their sombreros.

"*Buenas días,* Miguel," el Espectro greeted, addressing the *rurale* officer who led the patrol.

"And a good day to you, Rafael," Captain Garcia replied as he swung down from his mount. "I see you have already met Mr. Adams. I rode out here to tell you about him, but that appears to be unnecessary."

Clint swallowed hard. His heart seemed to stop from despair and hopelessness, but confusion and rage seemed to get it pumping again.

"Ah,"—the albino smiled as he turned to face

Clint—"I see our guest is puzzled. Why don't you explain it to him, Miguel."

"Very well," the captain agreed. "You see, Mr. Adams, el Espectro is Rafael Garcia. He is my brother."

TWENTY-FIVE

"Oh shit," the Gunsmith muttered. "Everything makes sense now."

"Adams is a very good detective," el Espectro told his brother. "Let's see what his deductions are, Miguel."

"I should have figured this out before," Clint commented. "Why are you building your headquarters less than a day's ride from a *rurale* fort? Because the *rurales* are your allies."

"Not *all* the *rurales* at Fort Juarez," Captain Garcia stated. "Just myself and these men here. One doesn't tell too many people a secret or it doesn't remain a secret for long."

"When I heard the Ghost speak English with the same New England accent as Garcia . . ." Clint shook his head. "I suppose this also explains how you managed to get all that fancy furniture for your office and those redwood doors?"

"Indeed," el Espectro confirmed. "A *rurale* officer can get anything if he has the money. Miguel and I share and share alike. I make the profits and he makes the connections. A nice little family business, eh?"

"Just like Cain and Abel," Clint muttered.

"Hardly," the Ghost scoffed. "All my life, Miguel

-121-

has been the one person I could call a friend. We have always been close. We always shall be."

"I haven't heard such a touching tale of love since I was told how vultures mate in midair," the Gunsmith sneered. "How long do you think it'll be before the *rurales* or the *federales* figure out what's going on?"

"Quite a while," Garcia answered. "I know how my superiors operate. They only put a fort here in the Devil's Belly because el Presidente Juarez has such a soft spot in his heart for the *peónes*. He wants them protected from the Yaqui and the *bandidos*. However, my superiors don't give a damn, Adams. I can do whatever I please in Sonora, providing I don't offend a politician or an aristocrat, and my commanders won't care."

"However, our arrangement here is only temporary," the albino added. "When the time is right, when we've acquired enough wealth and influence, Miguel and I plan to take up residence in Guatemala. We'll buy a coffee plantation and live like kings for the rest of our lives."

"Enough of this, Rafael," Garcia urged. "Kill this *gringo*. We have something more urgent to deal with."

"Adams has to tell us something before he dies," the Ghost declared. "He killed several of my men and then released my prisoners last night."

"I am aware your *peónes* have escaped," Garcia said sharply. "We encountered them on our way here."

"*Qué?*" the albino asked with surprise.

"There were about ten of them, men and women," the *rurale* captain explained. "When they saw us, they approached, probably looking for help. Then, Corporal Romero"—he turned and glared at one of his men—"stupidly opened fire on them. The *peónes* are armed with rifles and handguns. They fired back at us and we were forced to retreat."

"We have to find them," el Espectro said. "They can't get far on foot. I'll join you, Miguel. Together, with your men and mine, we'll easily take care of the peasant scum."

"*Sí*, Rafael," Garcia agreed. "It will be good to ride with you once again. What shall we do with Adams?"

"He has earned a slow and terrible death because he killed many of my men," the albino insisted. "But the *peónes* come first. Adams isn't going anywhere. I'll leave a couple men to look after him while we're gone."

"Very well," Garcia nodded. "But we'd better move quickly if we're going to catch those *peón* trash before they scatter all over Sonora."

"*Sí*," el Espectro agreed. He turned to his men. "Umberto! Franco!"

Two bandits rushed forward and their leader gave them some orders in rapid Spanish. The pair grinned wolfishly and nodded. The albino then addressed Clint Adams.

"I'm leaving these two to look after you while the rest of us hunt down the fugitives," he explained. "They are under orders not to kill you until we return because we all want to witness your death, Adams. Of course, they are allowed to entertain themselves at your expense."

Clint tried to think of an appropriate remark, but he didn't want to try to talk for fear his teeth would chatter.

"We shouldn't be gone long, Adams," el Espectro declared. "I hope my men don't get too carried away with their fun. Try not to die before we get back."

TWENTY-SIX

Chained to the whipping post, Clint Adams watched el Espectro, the majority of his *bandidos* and the five *rurales* mount their horses and ride from the camp. Umberto and Franco were left behind to guard the Gunsmith. Clint strained his muscles, pulling at the manacles that held him, but the iron shackles held fast.

Frustration boiled inside the Gunsmith like volcanic lava. If he could free himself, he'd only have to deal with two men. Clint couldn't hope for better odds than that, yet he was still powerless to act or even defend himself against whatever sadistic games his captors chose for "entertainment" until el Espectro and the others returned.

Umberto, a squat, fat *bandido* with a wide face and a mouthful of gold teeth, grinned as he approached Clint. "How you wanna spend time while we wait, *gringo*?" he asked in broken English.

"Do you fellas have a deck of cards?" the Gunsmith asked.

Umberto replied by slamming a fist into Clint's face. The Gunsmith's head recoiled from the blow and more blood streamed from his mouth.

"Take these manacles off and try that, *chico!*" Clint growled.

Umberto punched him in the stomach. The Gunsmith gasped as his breath spewed from his lungs. The bandit laughed and drew back his fist again.

"*Uno momento,*" the other bandit, Franco, urged.

The stocky beast turned to face his partner. He smiled when he saw the eight-foot-long bullwhip in Franco's hand. Clint cursed under his breath. He'd seen what a bullwhip can do to human flesh. The military seldom used punishment by flogging since too many men had been killed or crippled for life by the lash.

"*Sí*, Franco," Umberto nodded. "Let's teach this *gringo cochino* to rob us of our women!"

"Hey, where's your *machismo*, boys?" Clint shouted as the pair strode behind him. "Take these chains off and let's fight like men. You know what men are, don't you? Your mamas probably told you about them, unless the *putas* were too stupid to know how they got pregnant—"

The crack of the leather cord slicing through air interrupted the Gunsmith's insults. Then he felt the whip strike his naked back. Skin bruised and split open. Clint repressed a groan as he felt blood trickle from the cut flesh.

"*Cobardes!*" Clint snarled, still hoping to shame them into releasing him to fight on equal terms. "I'll take you both on at the same time. You little boys aren't afraid of one *gringo*, are you? You choose the weapons and—"

The lash struck again. Clint clenched his teeth and swallowed hard. Beads of cold sweat popped from his forehead and more blood oozed from ripped skin.

"No wonder you don't have the guts to fight me!" Clint yelled. "Can't you goddamn weaklings hit any harder than that?"

"*Sí, bastardo!*" Umberto's voice replied. "We will hit harder!"

Another loud crack pierced the air, but Clint's taut back didn't receive another blow from the bullwhip. He suddenly realized the sound had been the report of a rifle. He craned his neck to look over his shoulder at his tormentors.

Franco lay on the ground, the whip sprawled beside him. The bandit's hands were clamped over his lower abdomen as he convulsed in agony.

"*Cristo!*" Umberto exclaimed, dragging a pistol from its holster.

Another shot erupted and the fat *bandido* executed a clumsy backward run, blood oozing from his chest. A third rifle shot followed and a heavy lead slug hit the Mexican tub of lard in the throat. Umberto crashed to the ground.

"Clint!" a woman's voice cried. "Have those *cabróns* hurt you?"

Maria jogged toward him, carrying the Gunsmith's Springfield carbine. Smoke still curled from the muzzle of the weapon as she rushed to Clint's side.

"Oh! Your poor back!" she said. "I should have gut-shot *both* of them!"

"Make sure they're dead!" Clint told her.

Maria turned just in time to see Franco had managed to rise to one knee. He pawed at his holstered sidearm with one hand while the other tried to hold in his spilling intestines.

The girl worked the lever of the carbine and rapidly aimed it at the wounded bandit. The Springfield bellowed and one side of Franco's face vanished in a spray of blood and skull fragments.

"Good work!" the Gunsmith said. "Now, blast the links of this chain apart."

He pulled on a wrist manacle as far as he could, drawing the short chain to full length. Maria raised the carbine until the barrel rested on the frame of the whipping post. The muzzle almost touched the chain. Then she squeezed the trigger.

A 250-grain lead projectile burst the links apart. Tiny bits of metal bit into the Gunsmith's hand. He jerked his arm away from the post and yanked the broken chain free. Maria repeated the procedure and shot off the manacle at his other wrist. She aimed the carbine at the leg irons.

"Hold on, honey," Clint urged. "I'd just as soon not get shot in the foot. This is going to be a little tricky. Will you get me a revolver? Those dead fellas won't mind if you borrow one."

The girl hurried to the corpse of Umberto and returned with the bandit's pistol. Clint examined the gun and grunted sourly. It was a .44-caliber Walker-Colt cap-and-ball revolver. An awkward weapon with a poor trigger mechanism, it was nonetheless a powerful handgun.

Clint knelt and placed the gun lengthwise by his heel until the muzzle touched the chain of an ankle manacle. He cocked back the hammer and fired, splitting the iron links. Another bullet freed his left leg.

"Clint, they've hurt you!" Maria exclaimed, wrapping her arms around his neck.

The girl kissed his mouth hard, which would have been a pleasant experience if the Gunsmith's jaw didn't feel as if it had been used for a punching bag. Gently, he broke the embrace.

"Maria," Clint began "I'm mighty grateful to you for saving my life, but what the hell are you doing here?"

"A patrol of *rurales* attacked us . . ."

"I know," Clint said. "They're in league with el Espectro. What did you do after the *rurales* retreated?"

"Well, we had to run to the rocks for cover, of course, so after the *rurales* left, most of the others headed for San José. I saw your horse had run away during the gunfight, so I decided to try to find him. The animal led me back here. Then I saw el Espectro and the others ride out and I guessed you might need help."

"Woman's intuition." The Gunsmith smiled. "Hey, Duke must be close by!"

He whistled twice and a neigh replied. Duke galloped into the camp and whinnied as he trotted up to Clint. The Gunsmith patted the horse and Duke rubbed his muzzle against the man's chest.

"You've got a nose like a bloodhound, big fella." Clint grinned. "I'll be damned if you're not the best horse any man ever had."

Duke's head rose and lowered twice as if nodding in agreement. The Gunsmith laughed. "Well, I reckon you don't have to be modest, big fella."

"Your horse," Maria began, staring at Clint, "he understands you?"

"Sure," Clint shrugged. "But we'll talk about that later. Right now we've got to get the hell out of here. El Espectro and his men haven't been gone long and that means they've probably heard the shooting here. Ten to one, they're headed back this way and they'll be here any minute."

Duke nodded his head again and pawed the earth as if to say, "Right, let's move *fast!*"

TWENTY-SEVEN

"Marsha!" Clint exclaimed. "Marsha Woodland is still in the *hacienda*."

"Who?" Maria frowned.

"You'll see," he replied. "I can't leave without her. Come on."

The Gunsmith and Maria jogged to the *hacienda*. He quickly located el Espectro's office. The door was locked, but a .44 round from the confiscated Walker-Colt shattered the latch bolt. Clint slammed a bare foot into the door which abruptly swung open.

"Hot damn!" the Gunsmith declared when he saw his modified Colt .45 revolver, the New Line belly gun and the contents taken from his pockets—all neatly laid out on el Espectro's desk.

"Just like Christmas morning." Clint grinned.

He buckled on his gunbelt and put the .45 in its holster. There wasn't time to do anything with the rest of his belongings except stuff them into his pants pockets.

In the corridor, they discovered the Gunsmith's shirt, serape, sombrero and boots. Apparently, the *bandidos* had stripped him in the hallway. Clint grabbed his shirt and boots and continued down the corridor.

"Marsha!" he shouted. "Where the hell are you?

We're checking out of this bandit hotel!"

"Here I am!" a voice cried from behind one of the doors.

The sound of her fists banging on redwood led Clint to the right door. He aimed the Walker-Colt at the doorknob.

"Okay, Marsha," he announced. "I've found you. Now, stand clear of the door. I'm going to shoot the lock."

He fired. Wood splintered near the frame. A solid kick failed to budge the door. "One more time!" he shouted. The next shot broke the lock and a kick sent the door flying open.

Marsha Woodland dove into Clint's arms. "Oh, thank God!" she sobbed. "I thought I'd never get—"

"We've got to get out of here fast," Clint told her, tossing the empty cap-and-ball pistol aside.

"We can't get far on foot," Maria commented. She had gathered up Clint's sombrero and now placed it on his head. "And your horse can't carry all three of us."

"Nine of el Espectro's men have recently retired for good," the Gunsmith replied as he hastily pulled on his boots. "There ought to be at least two horses left in the corral. One for each of you ladies."

Clint slid into his shirt as he led them through the corridor and out the front door. Duke waited patiently for them while Clint located the corral. He found almost a dozen horses and quickly selected two that appeared strong and fit.

"We don't have time to put saddles on," Clint explained. "Just bridles and blankets."

"I can handle that," Marsha declared, proving she was familiar with horses.

While Marsha prepared the mounts for herself and

Maria, Clint relieved Franco's corpse of its gun—a .44-caliber Remington. Then he gathered up the bullwhip.

"Can you use a gun, Marsha?" he asked, draping the whip over his neck.

"If I have to," she replied. "Why are you taking that awful thing?"

"We might need a weapon that doesn't make as much noise as a gun. I've never been much for knives, but I've handled bullwhips before back in Texas. After a fella learns the wrist action, it's not too difficult to use one and it requires the same kind of distance judging and coordination as pistol shooting."

Two minutes later, Clint, Maria and Marsha galloped out of the bandit lair. They covered more than two miles without encountering el Espectro and his men. Clint brought Duke to a halt. The girls stopped their horses in response.

"I think we can slow down now," he announced. "No need to run our horses into the ground."

"We've escaped!" Maria smiled. "We've really gotten away from that white-faced *bastardo*!"

"Thank God," Marsha added, "it's finally over."

"Yeah," the Gunsmith agreed, although he knew it wasn't true.

TWENTY-EIGHT

"Now that we're free," Maria commented, "where do we go from here?"

"First we have to figure out where *here* is," Clint Adams replied.

The trio had ridden to an old arroyo surrounded by rock walls. The terrain bore a disturbing resemblance to the area where Clint and Juan Lopez had been ambushed by Yaqui Indians. The Gunsmith's hand never strayed from the grips of his pistol and he remained fully alert to any sign of danger as they rode through the pass.

"We're still in Sonora," Maria said slyly. "In el Barriga del Diablo. This area is called Catedral Negro—the Black Cathedral. That means we're about forty kilometers from the nearest village . . . namely, San José."

"We're going to Texas, aren't we?" Marsha asked urgently.

"Well"—Clint sighed—"we've got to cover some territory between here and there first. Besides, we've got to make a trip to San José anyway."

"But most of the *peónes* who escaped from the camp are from that village," Maria declared. "El Espectro will certainly head there if he fails to find the fugitives in the desert."

"That's exactly why we have to go there," the Gunsmith explained. "We can't just let the bandits swoop down on San José and slaughter every man, woman and child."

"But what can we do to save them?" Maria demanded.

"We'll figure that out when we get there," Clint answered.

"I want to go home!" Marsha sobbed. "Haven't we been through enough already?"

"Yeah," the Gunsmith agreed. "I've had my fill of bloodshed and violence. I've been strangled, beaten and whipped . . . and I know you ladies have been through a hell of a lot worse than that. But we still can't bury our heads in the sand and allow el Espectro to massacre an entire village. Not when there's a chance he can be stopped."

"You're going to get us killed, Clint," Maria said.

"Okay." The Gunsmith sighed. "What do we do if we don't go to San José? Do you think we can stay here and live on lizards and sagebrush in the middle of the goddamn desert?"

"It is possible," Maria replied. "I have done so myself."

Clint stared at her with surprise.

"Have you not noticed that I am unlike the other girls you found in the camp prison?" Maria inquired.

"Sure," Clint nodded. "You speak fluent English, you seem to know this desert like the back of your hand and you handle a gun and knife like you've had plenty of experience."

"I was once a *bandido's mujer*," she replied with a bitter smile. "His woman, no? He was the chief of a small band that lived in the Devil's Belly. Some time ago, el Espectro convinced my man's lieutenants that they should join his gang, which then consisted of about twenty members. Ricardo, my man, objected. So they killed him and I was one of his possessions which became communal property for the Ghost's private army."

"I really don't care if you used to be Satan's mistress," the Gunsmith told her. "You saved my life today and you're with us now. That's all that matters, Maria."

The Mexican beauty's dark eyes softened. She looked like she might cry. "Thank you, Clint."

He grinned back at her. "The sun is getting pretty low. Figure we'd better set up camp for the night?"

"*Sí*," Maria agreed.

"I don't really want to spend the night in a place like this," Marsha admitted. "But it can't be any worse than what we've already been through."

"Well, then—" the Gunsmith began, but a sudden movement by a boulder near the arroyo caught his attention.

The Gunsmith almost pulled his pistol before he recognized the brown-feathered figure that scurried into view. The prairie turkey, which resembled a large quail more than the bird beloved for Thanksgiving dinners, broke into an awkward run. Clint quickly urged Duke into a fast gallop.

Duke charged forward. The bird squawked and flapped its wings in a clumsy attempt at flight. Clint unslung the bullwhip from his neck and cocked back his arm. The turkey rose from the ground and the Gunsmith lashed out with the whip. Twisted black leather struck the bird on the neck. It fell from the sky in a tumbling somersault before crashing into a rock wall.

"*Magnífico!*" Maria exclaimed. "You are indeed

an expert with a whip, Clint."

"Expert is sort of a strong term," Clint replied modestly. "But we'll have a good dinner tonight. I'm sick of beef jerky and sardines."

They made camp near a large cave, a place Maria remembered from her days as a bandit's *mujer*. Clint fed and watered the horses while Marsha gathered some greasewood for the fire and Maria plucked the feathers from the dead turkey. Marsha finished her chores first and strolled toward the cave.

"Your Marsha is quite upset by her experience," Maria told Clint as she expertly slit open the turkey and scooped out its innards with the blade of her Bowie knife.

"She seems to be getting over it pretty well," the Gunsmith replied, draping the bullwhip over his shoulder.

"Not as well as it seems, Clint," Maria insisted. "There are some things a woman can tell about another woman better than a man can."

A piercing scream suddenly sounded from the cave. Clint dashed for the entrance and peered inside to see Marsha cowering by a rock wall. A seven-foot-long rattlesnake was coiled near her feet. Its ugly heart-shaped head was raised, forked tongue jutting in and out. The sinister rattle of its tail increased as the girl screamed again.

Clint dropped to one knee to compensate for the lack of space within the cave. He swung the whip in an overhead stroke. The lash whistled as it cut through the air before the lead-tipped end struck the rattler with explosive force. The snake's head burst apart and blood squirted between its eyes. Clint rushed to Marsha and took her hand, pulling her away from the reptile which thrashed about in wild death spasms.

"It's okay, Marsha—" Clint began, taking the girl in his arms.

"No!" she cried, pushing him away. "Don't touch me! No man is ever going to touch me ever again!"

Then she bolted outside.

Clint searched the cave for other snakes and such vermin as rats, scorpions and spiders. Finding none, he hauled out the dead rattler and declared the cave safe.

"I'm—I'm sorry about my behavior, Clint," Marsha said, not looking at him.

"Forget it," the Gunsmith replied. "But all men aren't like el Espectro and his bandits."

"Just leave me alone for a while," Marsha whispered. Then she buried her face in her hands and wept.

TWENTY-NINE

There was little conversation as the trio ate the prairie turkey Maria had prepared for dinner. Marsha ate little, but Clint's appetite was hearty enough and he consumed an ample portion of the meat.

"That was great, Maria," he told her as he wiped grease from his hands. "I'd like to see what you can do with a real kitchen to work in."

"I've fixed more meals on the prairie," Maria replied with a smile. "But maybe one day I'll prepare a real dinner for you."

"You've got a deal," the Gunsmith agreed.

"First we have to get out of this mess," Marsha said sourly.

"We will," Clint assured her. "Look, we were all prisoners of el Espectro's camp and now we're free and miles away from his headquarters. We know where we are and where we're going—"

"Yes!" Marsha snapped. "To an obscure Mexican village where you'll get us all killed fighting the bandits!"

"A priest in that obscure village helped me when I was trying to find el Espectro's lair to get you out of there," Clint told her in a hard voice. "A girl from that same village guided me the rest of the way. She also saved my life. You'd still be a prisoner if it hadn't been for them, Marsha. We owe those people."

The girl did not reply. She rose without saying a word and placed a blanket on the ground. Obviously, she didn't relish the idea of going back inside the cave. Marsha wrapped the blanket around herself like a cocoon. Minutes later, she was sound asleep.

"Poor kid's exhausted," Clint remarked.

"It has been a long day for us all," Maria added. "Do we sleep in shifts? Perhaps divide the night into two four-hour watches?"

"I doubt if el Espectro is going to try to track us in the dark," Clint said. "But if any danger arrives, Duke will let us know. He can hear better than humans can and he can smell trouble a mile away."

"He is quite a horse," Maria agreed. "Then why don't we get some rest, my hero?"

"Sounds good," he nodded.

Clint picked up his bedroll, uncertain where to put it—on the ground or in the cave. Maria solved the problem by whispering, "The cave, Clint. We will have more privacy there, no?"

The Gunsmith agreed. Maria strode into the cave and Clint followed. By the time he'd laid down the bedroll, the girl had slipped out of her tattered dress and began washing her body with a canteen and cloth.

"The smell of a woman pleases a man," she remarked. "But not when she smells too strong, no?"

Clint smiled, watching her. Maria's body was lovely. Her breasts were large and firm with hard brown nipples. Maria's torso was sleek and tan and her hips flared before tapering into long, shapely legs. The Gunsmith wasn't too tired to appreciate a beautiful woman and his manhood stirred with anticipation.

He removed his clothing as he watched Maria. As soon as he'd stripped off his long johns, Maria was in his arms, her wide moist mouth pressed against his. Her hands found his penis and stroked it to full length. Clint fondled her breasts, gently thumbing the nipples erect. He lowered his head and kissed the soft, warm flesh.

Clint drew on Maria's nipples, sucking gently as his hands continued down the curves of her body. Two fingers found the wet, hot portal of love. He rubbed and probed slowly. Maria moaned with pleasure, rocking her buttocks back and forth to the rhythm of his touch.

"Lie down, my hero," she urged. "Let me show you how a woman should treat her man."

The Gunsmith obliged. He clenched his teeth and winced when his back touched the blanket draped over the rough ground. The wounds he'd received from the flogging were still raw and painful although he'd applied a camphor ointment when they'd made camp. He realized he'd probably have to repeat the treatment after he spent some time with Maria—but, hell, it'd be worth it.

Maria knelt beside him and slowly ran her hands over his hairy chest and abdomen. She lowered her lips to his neck and shoulders. Clint sighed with pleasure as she kissed and gently nipped his flesh. Gradually, her mouth moved to his chest. Maria's hands found his hardened penis and stroked it carefully while she kissed his bare stomach.

A shiver of erotic glee traveled through Clint as she slowly traced the tip of her tongue around his navel. Her mouth continued to move until she slipped her lips over the head of his penis. She licked, chewed and sucked with passion and skill until Clint was about to reach his limit.

Then Maria raised her head and shifted a leg over his loins to straddle him. She guided his member into her love center. They sighed in unison when he entered her. The girl wiggled her loins against Clint, working his hard cock deeper. Clint pressed the backs of his heels against the ground as he arched his back to add thrust to his penetration.

Maria, in the dominant position, handled the role with enthusiasm and skill. She stroked his chest, ribs and abdomen with one hand, while the other was thrust under her own buttocks until her fingers found his testicles. Maria rocked her body gently, her featherlike touch massaging his balls as she moved.

The girl moaned and gradually began bobbing her body up and down, riding the length of Clint's throbbing, stiff shaft. The Gunsmith bucked his body in rhythm to hers and Maria gasped with pleasure when his member plunged deep inside her.

Clint felt himself reaching the peak of his endurance as Maria clenched her teeth to hold in a scream of delight. At last, the woman quivered in a tremendous orgasm and Clint blasted his hot, creamy load into Maria's magnificent womb.

"Oh, my hero," she sobbed. "It has been so long since I have done this willingly. I had almost forgotten how good it can be."

"Then we'll have to make certain this night is vivid enough to sustain you for a while," Clint replied.

THIRTY

The trio continued their journey after dawn. There had still been no sign of el Espectro or evidence that he had followed them into the Black Cathedral. Yet, this did not prove they weren't being pursued, only that the bandits had not yet caught up with them.

Neither the Gunsmith nor his female companions relaxed as they rode. If el Espectro had managed to reach San José first, he could have already destroyed the village. The bandits might be waiting for Clint to return to San José, or if el Espectro knew the terrain, he may have already sent men into the Negro Catedral to lie in wait for the Gunsmith.

Every rock formation and boulder seemed sinister, a potential hiding place for *bandido* assailants or hostile Yaqui Indians. Clint gazed over the natural walls of stone. Outgrowths of rock and clusters of stone on ledges could provide perfect cover. *An ideal spot for an ambush*, the Gunsmith thought grimly, his hand resting on the grips of his holstered Colt revolver.

After two hours that seemed like decades of sheer tension, they emerged from the Black Cathedral. The bare, featureless terrain of the desert was almost a relief. The Gunsmith checked his canteens. One was empty, the other less than half full. *If we don't find water by noon* . . . Clint thought. *Well, I hope*

Maria's right about her directions. I'd rather go to San José and fight el Espectro than die of thirst out here.

His concern was needless for they reached San José later that morning. The villagers saw them approach and excited shouts summoned everyone into the center of the hamlet. Most of the *peónes* cheered and waved sombreros in welcome. A few waved rifles or revolvers overhead. Others didn't appear to be pleased by the Gunsmith's return.

Clint spotted two members of the crowd he especially welcomed—Father Rameriz and Elena Jimenez. The Gunsmith dismounted and the lovely little Mexican girl flew into his arms. She kissed him hard on the mouth. Voices cheered once more. Someone sighed, *"Estar enamorado!"*

"Oh, Clint!" Elena said. "I feared you might not return. *Gracias a Dios!* You are here!"

"Welcome back, my friend," Father Rameriz said, extending a hand. "Elena and the others arrived last night. They had quite a story to tell about you, my son."

"Unfortunately," Clint replied, taking the priest's hand, "we haven't come to the end yet."

"You too believe el Espectro will come in search of his escaped prisoners," Rameriz said grimly. He wasn't asking a question.

"I *know* he will, Father. After all, he sent out a search party when Elena was the only fugitive. Now his security is in even greater jeopardy."

"From what Elena told me," the priest remarked, "el Espectro seemed to have little regard for the security of his camp. He was surrounded by a half-built wall and posted guards only on his prisoners, without stationing sentries to patrol the perimeter of his base. I am not a military man, but this seems most careless to me."

"Your observations are accurate as usual, Father." Clint smiled. "But el Espectro wasn't being as careless as it may seem. The bandit's real name is Rafael Garcia. His brother is Captain Garcia. With the *rurale* boss as an ally, why would the Ghost be worried about an assault?"

"*Madre de Dios!*" Rameriz shook his head. "That explains why the *rurales* attacked Elena and the others. It also means we can not go to Fort Juarez for help for they too are our enemies."

"Not all of them, Father," Clint explained. "Garcia told me that just he and the four men with him on patrol are dealing with the bandits. The bastard thought I was going to die so he probably told the truth."

"But how could the other *rurales* remain ignorant of this for so long?" Rameriz asked.

"Well, we don't know how long el Espectro has had his headquarters in the Devil's Belly," Clint answered. "He still doesn't have his damn wall built, so I don't think he's been there much more than six months or so. He's been operating in Mexico for years, but I bet he didn't set up here until his brother took over command of Fort Juarez."

The priest nodded. "And that was about eight months ago."

"As for keeping the secret from his men," Clint continued, "that wouldn't be too difficult for the post commander to do. He probably sent out patrols to certain areas, purposely sending only his personal henchmen when it required approaching the bandit lair. The others were always sent in the opposite direction."

"*Sí*," the priest agreed. "It would be possible at

that. It must be or this could not be happening."

"What matters now," Elena said, "is what are we going to do?"

"The *rurales*?" Rameriz asked.

"They're too far away to help now," Clint replied. "Before we could reach Fort Juarez, the bandits would catch up with us."

"Besides," Maria added, "how can we convince them that their post commander is in league with el Espectro? What proof do we have?"

"That isn't a problem," Clint told her. "We've got ample evidence. Right, Marsha?"

"Yes," the blonde confirmed. "I can tell them what happened and that your claims are true . . . if they'd listen."

"They will," Clint assured her. "Your father is a congressman and no *rurale* officer is going to dismiss your word—not with El Presidente Juarez in office."

"This is a minor point," Rameriz sighed. "As you say, Clint, there is not time to go to Fort Juarez."

"I'm afraid not. There's only one way to deal with el Espectro and his gang. We'll have to fight them ourselves."

"You are a bold man, my son," Rameriz said. "A true warrior. Yet, the people of this village are farmers. They are not prepared to fight a small army of *bandidos*."

"Thirty-five men aren't exactly an army," Clint stated.

"They are to us," Rameriz insisted. "The *bandidos* are well armed and familiar with violence."

"And they're bullies, not soldiers," Clint told him. "They're not used to having anyone hit back at them. Your people have a few rifles and revolvers . . ."

"*Sí,*" the priest admitted. "They took the guns from the bodies of dead *bandidos*. That doesn't mean they know how to fight with such weapons."

"They'll fight," Maria declared.

She took Clint's face in her hands and kissed him fiercely on the mouth, purposely rubbing her body against his crotch. Then Maria turned and smiled coyly at Elena who looked furious. She stepped toward the center of the village and began shouting at the *peónes*. Although Clint could understand little of what she said, her Spanish contained a taunting quality and she held her hands on her hips in a defiant manner.

The *peónes* stared at her in astonishment as she drew her Bowie knife and held the blade high. Maria turned and pointed at Elena and continued to address the citizens of San José in a snide voice. Then she pointed at "Señor Clint" and said something about him.

"What's she saying?" Clint asked Rameriz.

"She told them they have to fight," the priest answered. "She said that she has killed el Espectro's men with a gun and with a knife. Even 'little Elena' has killed the *bandido* scum. She says, 'If you call yourselves men, then you too will fight and Señor Clint will lead you.' She tells them to follow you, my son, because you are wise, brave and good."

The Gunsmith noticed many *peónes* staring at him with expectation and hope in their eyes. Others seemed embarrassed, shamed by their fear. Then other former prisoners of el Espectro's camp spoke to them. They gestured at Clint and pointed at themselves with pride. Obviously, they were telling elaborate war stories about their escape from the bandits' clutches and their battle with the *rurales*.

"Maria," Clint called to the girl, "don't let these

fellas get too confident. We don't want them to be too scared to fight, but we don't want them to go into combat with the idea this is going to be a turkey shoot either. Underestimating an enemy is a surefire way to get killed."

"I'll tell them, my hero," Maria replied with a smile, pleased that she'd been chosen as Clint's spokesperson instead of Elena.

The younger woman also noticed this and glared at Clint. The Gunsmith didn't have time to explain to her that he wasn't favoring Maria because he felt more for her than he did for Elena—and in fact, he couldn't have honestly said which woman he liked more—but Maria was older and her personality was more commanding. She wasn't a *peón* and her manner was neither submissive nor shy. The men would listen to her, but they'd be inclined to ignore "little Elena."

Too many lives were at stake to be concerned with either woman's ego. Clint had to concentrate on the main problem that threatened every man, woman and child of San José—el Espectro. Father Rameriz placed a hand on Clint's shoulder.

"I am not a man of violence, my son," the priest said. "But we have no choice. If we do not fight, el Espectro will slaughter us. Perhaps we can not win, but at least we can die like rams instead of sheep, no?"

"Rams butt heads out in the open," Clint replied. "If we try to fight the bandits on their terms, we'll be shot to pieces. What you said about our side being largely inexperienced and not as well armed as the enemy is true, Father. We have to take on el Espectro in a manner that will compensate for these disadvantages."

"But how will we do that, Clint?" Rameriz asked.

"We pick the battleground," the Gunsmith told him. "Not here. San José wasn't built for an ambush. We'd be cut to ribbons here."

"Then where . . . ?" the puzzled priest began.

"I know just the place," Clint smiled.

THIRTY-ONE

When the Gunsmith and the people of San José arrived at the Negro Catedral several of the superstitious *peónes* crossed themselves and muttered prayers as they stared up at the rock formations with dread. Clint saw this and reported their behavior to Father Rameriz.

"Will you tell your people not to be afraid of this place?" Clint urged, wrapping the bullwhip around his neck. "Tell them the walls of stone are not evil. Didn't God make the rocks? Is it just a coincidence that this place is a natural fortress that will provide us with ample cover when we fight the *bandidos?*"

"Your point is well made, my son," the priest agreed. "The Devil is not a builder. He can only tempt, mislead and influence. He is the Prince of Lies, not the Creator. There is no evil on earth unless man brings it upon himself."

"I'm glad to have you here to talk to them about this, but I still wish we could have found some safe place for you and some of the others."

"The old ones and the children?" Rameriz sighed. "I am a blind man so I am also a burden on a battlefield."

"You're a very brave and remarkable man, Father," Clint said. "But you can't see and that's one hell of a drawback when it comes to trading bullets."

"This is true, my son." The priest smiled. "But you may yet be glad I am here."

"Clint?" Maria called to him as she strode forward. "We've only got six rifles, eleven pistols and one shotgun. There's very little ammo and what we do have is limited to forty-five and forty-four calibers."

"It wouldn't help much to reload anyway," Clint declared. "Not with inexperienced *peónes* against seasoned *bandidos*. If we don't take them out with the first attack—or at least cut down their number dramatically—they'll swarm over the rocks before our people can deal with it. They're not trained well enough to handle a sudden change in tactics and we don't have time to teach them. This *has* to work the first time."

"Why did you encourage them to bring their machetes and sickles?" Maria asked.

"If it comes to hand-to-hand fighting," Clint explained, "they'll do better with knives and tools they're familiar with rather than trying to use a rifle butt at close quarters."

"How can you be certain el Espectro will even pass through the Black Cathedral?" Father Rameriz asked.

"I'm not," the Gunsmith confessed. "That's why we had to evacuate the village. It's possible he'll approach San José from another direction. I don't like exposing kids and old folks to danger, but the bandits would massacre them if they were left in the village alone and el Espectro showed up."

"But you think he will come this way?" the priest inquired.

"Yes, I do," Clint replied. "The way I figure it, el Espectro didn't track Elena and the others or he would have already hit San José by now. That means he heard the gunshots when Maria rescued me from the two mad dogs he'd left at the camp. He must have headed back there, found we'd already left—with Marsha, his yellow-haired prize—and decided to hunt us down first. If I'm right, he's probably only a couple hours behind us—he could arrive here at any minute."

"That means we must prepare swiftly, my son," Rameriz stated.

"That's already being taken care of," Clint assured him. "We've moved the horses to a semicircle of rocks away from the main walls. All the animals except Duke have been ground-hobbled to keep them from wandering about and giving away our position."

"And your horse will not wander?" the priest asked.

"He'll stay put unless I call for him. I'm stationing the men with rifles—"

"The *men*?" Maria inquired stiffly.

"Okay, you'll be there too." Clint sighed. "Anyway, I'm putting everyone with a rifle on both sides of the pass, positioning them high on the rock walls to put the bandits in a crossfire. However, the men with pistols—"

"Don't forget me, Clint," Marsha Woodland declared. She held a revolver in her fist.

"I told you I don't want you involved in this," the Gunsmith replied.

"I know how to shoot," she insisted. "And I've got a personal score to settle with those bastards. I'm going to kill some *bandidos* today, Clint. That's all there is to it."

"Aw, hell," Clint muttered. "Okay, the *folks* with pistols will be stationed on one side only. Men—I guess I can say that this time—armed only with machetes and sickles will also be at that rock wall. The others, in charge of our surprise, will be at the summit of the opposite cliff."

"Your strategy sounds good in theory, my son," Rameriz commented. "I hope it will serve as well in actual practice."

"We'll know when el Espectro and his men arrive," the Gunsmith said. "Right now, we have to get everybody in position."

"Perhaps I can help you know when the bandits are coming," the priest remarked.

Rameriz raised his stave, which now featured a sharpened end, and drove the point into the ground hard. Then he knelt beside it and clamped his teeth around the shaft. Everyone except the Gunsmith and Maria thought his actions were bizarre and irrational.

"They're not close yet," the priest declared.

"How—" Marsha began. "What are you doing, Father?"

"A simple matter of vibrations, my daughter," Rameriz explained. "You see, sound and vibrations actually travel through dense matter better than they do through the lighter substance of air. This is why one can hear a noise at sea for such a great distance, because it is carried by the denser substance of water. If one *listens* to the ground, the vibrations naturally carry better through this even denser matter than they do at sea. The Indians have known this for centuries."

"Why do you put the stick in your teeth?" Marsha asked. "Wouldn't it be better if you placed your ear to the ground?"

"No," Rameriz said. "You see, the stick serves to increase the reception of vibrations, since it is a dense object driven into the ground to pick up shock waves.

As for putting my teeth on it, the vibrations carry through the stick and into my teeth and jaw. In fact, they even carry up to my ear. I'll be able to *feel* and *hear* the bandits approach."

"And since Father Rameriz is more sensitive to sounds and vibrations," Clint added, "he's better suited for the task than a sighted person."

"Exactly." The priest grinned. "A blind lookout. Ironic is it not?"

"I have absolute faith in your ability," the Gunsmith assured him.

I just wish I could feel the same way about a bunch of scared farmers who have never tried to fight back until today, he thought. *Let's pray for some beginner's luck.*

A lot of it.

THIRTY-TWO

Although frightened and filled with self-doubt about their new roles as warriors, the *peónes* from San José did have one attribute of good soldiers—they obeyed orders. When Clint checked the rock walls, he found everyone stationed exactly where he'd told them to be, even though they would obviously have preferred to be someplace else, doing something else.

Clint couldn't blame them for that because he felt the same way.

Of course, when it was over—provided he survived—the Gunsmith would return to Brookstown, Texas and collect his two thousand dollars from Andrew Woodland. The congressman was also going to give five hundred dollars to the widow of Juan Lopez or Clint would turn the man upside down and shake him until the money fell out of his pockets. Juan had paid the ultimate price, and by God, his death would not be in vain. In fact, the Gunsmith had also decided to give Mrs. Lopez a thousand from his own reward money as well.

In the meantime, he had to do his best to keep Marsha Woodland from getting her pretty head shot off.

Clint found the lovely young blonde positioned behind a boulder on a ledge. The big rock provided good cover and she still had a revolver taken from one of the dead bandits—the .44-caliber Remington, a good handgun. Now, if only she wouldn't lose her head and get careless when the shooting began.

"You look like you're set up pretty well, Marsha," the Gunsmith commented.

"I'm ready for el Espectro," she replied.

"That's good," Clint grinned. " 'Cause I'm not."

"How much longer do you think we'll have to wait?"

"It shouldn't be very long, Marsha," he replied. "When it's over, we'll head back to Texas and you'll be home again."

"Maybe I won't go home," she said stiffly. "Home is really Washington, D.C., you know. It's full of stupid, smiling young men who pretend to be cultured and gentle. But now I know what they're really like. . . ."

"Figure you'll join a convent?" Clint asked dryly.

"I don't know yet." Marsha glanced up at him. "I don't know what I'll do, but don't worry. I'll make sure my father rewards you for bringing me back to him . . . if we get back."

"We will," he assured her. "And when we get back, you'd do well to stop judging all men by el Espectro and his bandits. I've known some women who were pretty vicious and deceitful, but I haven't—"

"Did any of them ever rape you?" Marsha sneered.

"In a way," Clint replied. "The spirit can be raped as badly as the body, Marsha. A man can be used and lied to by a woman. He can be hurt here"—Clint touched his chest near the heart—"and that's not easy to deal with, Marsha. What it gets down to is whether

BANDIDO BLOOD

you learn to live with that hurt and try again, or spend the rest of your life alone. Don't deny yourself a second chance, Marsha. There really are some good people in this world."

"I—I guess I'll just need some time," the girl said softly.

"I understand," Clint said. "You take care of yourself and don't take any foolish chances. Everything is going to be okay."

"Will *anything* ever be okay again?" she asked herself.

"In time, Marsha," he assured her. "In time."

Poor Marsha. She was an incredibly beautiful girl and she seemed to be bright, resourceful and courageous. However, the ordeal with the bandits had scarred her personality and would prevent her from enjoying a loving relationship with a man if she didn't overcome it.

Of course, Marsha had been raised in a more genteel environment than Maria, who had formerly been a bandit's mistress, or Elena, who was accustomed to the harsh life of a *peón*, which had included abuse from *bandidos* and soldiers. Considering her background, Marsha had come through the experience quite well. In time, she'd probably recover and she'd be a stronger, more understanding person after having conquered a damn hard emotional struggle.

It's the hard times that build character, Clint had long ago decided. *And if we all live through the next few hours there'll be some solid gold characters in this god-forsaken place.*

Clint Adams climbed along the face of the cliff to his own prearranged battle station. The site was on a ledge with a cluster of cone-shaped rocks near the base of the wall. It featured good cover, but it was close to the arroyo, which meant Clint would be near the bandits when they entered the pass.

He'd chosen the site because he wanted to be certain of being within effective pistol range. Maria still had Clint's Springfield and the only weapons he carried were his .45, the New Line holdout gun and the bullwhip. Neither of the latter weapons were suited for a full-scale gun battle and Clint could only rely on the modified Colt when the shooting began. However, the Gunsmith was an expert's expert with a pistol and he intended to make every shot count.

Clint gazed down at Father Rameriz who was once again positioned by his stave, teeth clenched around the shaft, "listening" for the approach of enemy horses. The Gunsmith admired and respected Rameriz, but he hoped the priest would have ample time to reach the cover of the rocks before the bandits reached the pass. How fast could he move without eyes to guide him?

Something moved at the rocks beside Clint and he turned to find Elena Jimenez had climbed to his position. The girl's marvelous dark eyes glared at Clint and her wide, lush mouth formed a full-lipped pout.

"Maria thinks you are her man," Elena declared. "Is that true?"

"Jesus," Clint rasped. "This isn't the time to talk about personal relationships—"

"Are you her man?" Elena demanded.

"I'm my own man," he replied. "I don't belong to you or Maria or anyone else."

She clung to his arm. "Do you think I am too young? I am not a child, Clint. I am a woman and I will please you as no other can."

"I know you're a woman," Clint assured her. "And if you want to please me, you'll get back to your station and wait."

"I will show you," she insisted, throwing one arm around his neck.

Elena's lips clamped over Clint's in a fiery kiss, her tongue sliding inside his mouth. Her other hand fell to his crotch and fumbled with the buttons of his fly. The Gunsmith immediately responded to the kiss, his own passion already heated by her actions. Clint mentally told himself to stop and managed to get his body to oblige.

"Elena . . ." he began, breaking the kiss.

Before he could stop the girl, Elena had dropped to her knees and quickly took his now erect member in her mouth. Her hands clawed into his thighs for a firm grip as she drew on him gently, flicking her tongue along the head of his shaft.

"Jesus . . ." Clint moaned, unable to deny the intense pleasure he felt as her lips slid down the length of his penis.

When he'd first met Elena, he'd wondered what her wide, cushiony lips would be like. He'd wanted to kiss her even then and to feel his throbbing cock deep inside that beautiful mouth.

The girl was doing a hell of a job at making reality even better than fantasy. Elena may have lacked Maria's experience, but she had a lot of natural talent and plenty of passion. Elena continued to ride her lips along his manhood, gradually increasing the speed and sucking harder.

"Elena, you'd better—" he tried to warn her.

The young girl responded by moving her head back and forth even faster. Clint could no longer contain himself. Hot, creamy semen erupted in Elena's mouth. She accepted it without objection and milked him of the last drop with her wide, strong lips.

"The *bandidos* are coming!" Father Rameriz announced.

"Reckon it's their turn," Clint muttered.

THIRTY-THREE

"Damn it, Elena!" Clint growled, stuffing his penis back inside his trousers with his left hand as his right reached for the Colt. "Get to your post!"

"*Sí, amor mio,*" the girl replied quickly. "Take care, Clint."

Then she scrambled up the face of the cliff like a human mountain goat. The Gunsmith turned to the arroyo and saw Father Rameriz heading for the rocks. His concern for the priest proved needless. Rameriz moved in a quick shuffling gait, his stave swinging to and fro at the ground in front of him to guide his way. Rameriz reached shelter in a matter of seconds.

The last few minutes of waiting were the worst. The Gunsmith felt a familiar cold ball knot in his stomach, a combination of fear and excitement. His mouth was dry, but he no longer tasted the metallic flavor of terror when confronting death. He'd seen its skull-face too many times before. Clint Adams had long ago accepted the fact that a violent death awaited him. All he asked was to die fighting like a man with a gun in his hand.

The sound of approaching horse hooves rumbled within the Black Cathedral, the sound echoing along the rock walls where the Gunsmith and his ragtag army waited. At last, the first two figures on horseback rode into view. They wore uniforms and badges on their sombreros. Were they two of Captain Garcia's henchmen or part of an innocent *rurale* patrol which had wandered into the area?

The answer followed. Three dozen riders appeared behind the *rurales*. Most wore the dusty clothing, bandoliers and shaggy-beast faces of *bandidos*. Among their ranks rode el Espectro astride his great white stallion as well as Captain Garcia and the other two corrupt *rurales*.

Pretty clever, Mr. Ghost, the Gunsmith thought. *Sending the rurales ahead to serve as point men. That's a good way to catch any random travelers off guard. But why is he using point men? Does he suspect a trap? I noticed this was a perfect spot for an ambush. Has el Espectro done likewise? Does he have a plan of action? Is it better than ours?*

Clint chided himself for such thoughts. It was too late to change tactics now. They'd have to go through with what they'd prepared for and pray it worked.

"Just a little farther," Clint whispered, his finger on the trigger of the Colt, thumb resting on its hammer.

The bandits obliged and kept riding until they reached the center of the arroyo—flanked on both sides by the rock walls that concealed the Gunsmith's forces.

Now! Clint thought.

As if responding to a telepathic command, the *peónes* stationed on the summit of the opposite wall applied the shafts of picks and hoes to boulders. They used the tools for levers and pried the big rocks until man and stone groaned from the effort. The bandits heard the sound and glanced up to see three huge spheres of stone topple forward.

"*Derrumbe!*" screamed several voices.

The boulders plunged into other rocks and stony

ledges that broke from the impact and tumbled down the face of the cliff. Hundreds of rocks showered down on el Espectro's gang. Some were no larger than pebbles, others were as big as a horse's head. Men screamed as the hail of rocks pelted them, breaking bone and splitting skin.

Several dazed *bandidos* toppled from their mounts. Horses shrieked in pain and fear as they too were bombarded by the lethal shower. Cannonball-size projectiles shattered skulls and caved in chests. Then the trio of boulders came crashing down.

One crushed a stunned figure in a *rurale* uniform before it slammed into the legs of a bandit's horse, bowling over the animal and its rider before smashing them both. Another boulder landed directly on a mounted bandit, squashing the man and breaking the backbone of his unfortunate horse. The third rolled to the opposite rock wall where two terrified *bandidos* had fled. The giant stone mashed them into a bloody pulp, grinding their bodies against the wall.

No sooner had the avalanche occurred than a volley of sniper fire followed. The *peónes* armed with rifles, stationed high at both sides of the pass, opened fire on the disoriented, dazed bandits. Most of the bullets failed to claim human targets, but some tore into *bandidos*, sending more of el Espectro's followers to the Great Chili Festival in Hell.

Clint held his Colt revolver in both hands and aimed carefully before he squeezed the trigger and blasted a .45 round into the only corrupt *rurale* flunky still on his feet. Blood splashed the man's uniform tunic and he collapsed in a lifeless heap. The Gunsmith swung his pistol toward a *bandido* still on horseback and shot him out of the saddle.

He caught a glimpse of el Espectro, still mounted on his white stallion. A *peón* boldly, if foolishly, charged the Ghost, waving a machete overhead. El Espectro aimed a revolver at the man and shot him in the face. Clint prepared to open fire on the bandit boss, but two Mexican outlaws had spotted his position and suddenly blasted a volley of lead at the Gunsmith.

Clint ducked behind the stone cones, hearing bullets ricochet off rock. Then he thrust his gun arm between two stalagmites and returned fire with three double-action .45 rounds. The two bandits twisted as the slugs punched into their chests. Their tequila drinking days were over. They slumped to the ground and died.

Although bullets hissed through the air and more bandits fell, others still survived the ambush. They ran in all directions, some attempting to flee while others charged the rock walls.

The *bandidos* who retreated discovered their opponents were not in a merciful mood. Sniper bullets tore into their backs and pitched them into awkward somersaults—clumsy, acrobatic dances of Death. Some of the bandits who charged the rocks were cut down by pistol fire. The rest soon found themselves engaged in fierce close-quarters combat with the *peónes*.

Three farmers armed with machetes and sickles attacked a pair of pistol-packing bandits. El Espectro's men opened fire and two *peónes* fell. The third lived long enough to reach his assailants. His machete slashed and the blade struck a bandit in the side of the neck. The man's head popped off and a fountain of blood bubbled from the stump of his neck. The other bandit backed away from his decapitated partner, his face a mask of horror. Clint Adams then delivered the man's final judgment by pumping a .45 slug into his heart.

A bandit screamed and plunged headlong from an overhang of rock, a peasant's sickle lodged between his shoulder blades. Several *peónes* threw rocks at the approaching bandits and more followers of el Espectro toppled to the ground with bashed-in faces and bleeding skulls.

Father Rameriz butt-stroked a bandit in the face with the shaft of his stave. The stunned bandit fell on his back and the priest, guided by the sound of his adversary's body striking the ground, drove the sharpened end of his stick into the man's chest.

Another *bandido* swung a gun toward Rameriz, but Clint fired first. The bandit's sombrero hopped into the sky when a .45 bullet crashed into the back of his skull.

A *peón* leaped onto the back of a bandit, grabbing his arms and holding the outlaw long enough for another farmer to slam the point of a sickle blade into the man's stomach. *Peónes* gathered up firearms, dropped by dead and wounded bandits, and opened fire on the few members of el Espectro's gang who hadn't already been dispatched to the Gates of Bandido Hell.

Clint Adams opened the loading gate of his revolver to remove the spent cartridges when he saw two figures on horseback gallop past his position.

"Shit!" he exclaimed.

El Espectro and Captain Garcia were about to escape and the Gunsmith's Colt was out of ammunition.

THIRTY-FOUR

There wasn't time to reload his pistol or reach inside his shirt for the .22 New Line Colt. Clint hastily laid down his empty revolver and swung the bullwhip from his shoulder. The braided leather snaked out like a great black tentacle and struck the *rurale* captain under the chin.

The whip curled around Garcia's neck. Clint pulled hard and yanked the captain out of the saddle. Garcia toppled over the rump of his horse and fell to the ground hard.

"*Bastardo!*" el Espectro snarled as he turned in his saddle and aimed a pistol at the Gunsmith.

Clint's whip lashed out once more. The leather cord snared the Ghost's weapon and plucked it from his white bony fingers. El Espectro dug his spurs into his stallion's flesh and the horse galloped away like a bolt of ivory lightning.

The Gunsmith leaped down from his station and whistled loudly. Duke heard the sound and immediately charged forward. Clint tossed the whip aside and dug the New Line Colt from his shirt as the big gelding approached.

Captain Garcia groaned and slowly began to sit up, his hand reaching for a button-flap holster on his hip. Clint stepped forward and kicked Garcia in the face. The *rurale* slumped unconscious. The Gunsmith swiftly caught the horn of Duke's saddle and hauled himself onto the horse's back.

"Get that snow-white son of a bitch, big boy!" Clint rasped, pulling the reins to point Duke's head toward the fleeing form of el Espectro and his stallion.

Duke exploded in a dead run, racing after the albino like a greyhound chasing a rabbit. The big gelding's long legs covered ground rapidly, but el Espectro's stallion was also a strong, fast horse and the Ghost continued to gallop away.

"We can do it, fella," Clint urged, holding the reins in one hand and the diminutive .22 in the other. "I have to get close to use this peashooter, so catch up with 'em, fella."

Perhaps the horse didn't understand his rider, but Duke burst into an even faster run nonetheless. The white horse galloped around the base of a rock butte, with Duke coming up behind him fast.

Clint tried to aim the New Line Colt at el Espectro's black-cowled figure. Trying to shoot accurately at a fast moving object while mounted on a galloping horse was impossible even for the Gunsmith, especially when armed with a short-barreled .22 pistol designed for close quarters. He fired anyway, not expecting to hit the bandit. Clint aimed high, not wanting to hit the magnificent white stallion, hoping only to disorient its rider.

El Espectro recoiled violently in the saddle. Clint was surprised since he had been certain his bullet had missed. The albino yanked back on the reins and brought his mount to an abrupt halt. Then he toppled out of the saddle to the ground. Duke almost galloped past the white horse before Clint brought the big black Arabian to a standstill.

He turned in the saddle and saw el Espectro dash

around the rear of his stallion. The albino, who clearly had only pretended to be wounded, charged toward Clint before the Gunsmith could adjust the aim of his New Line. White talons seized Clint's arm and yanked him forcibly off Duke's back.

Clint managed to land on his feet and remained upright despite the powerful tug exercised by his opponent. He slammed his left fist into the side of el Espectro's head, but the albino seemed to absorb the blow without effect. He twisted Clint's arm fiercely and the little Colt sprang from his grasp. Clint saw the gun land beside a clump of multicolored rock that resembled a large piece of coral.

El Espectro's steel-clawed hand suddenly seized Clint's throat. Well aware of the strength in his adversary's fingers, the Gunsmith desperately struggled to break free. He pried at the Ghost's wrist with his left hand and rammed a knee into his groin. El Espectro gasped and snarled like a beast, but his grip at Clint's throat remained firm.

Then he pulled Clint off balance and the Gunsmith landed on his back with the murderous albino on top of him. The Gunsmith's right arm was held immobile by a powerful hand, and a knee quickly pinned his left. El Espectro's fingers continued to squeeze Clint's throat, the pressure threatening to crush his windpipe.

"I should have finished you off before, Adams," the albino hissed, his teeth clenched in rage. The Gunsmith could only imagine what the man's red-tinted eyes were like as they were still covered by the thick, dark glasses. "But today you die . . ."

Clint bent a knee and whipped it up as high as he could, striking el Espectro in the left kidney. The Ghost groaned and buckled from the unexpected blow. Clint shoved his captive right wrist against the albino's thumb and broke free of the grip. His hand shot out quickly, clawing at el Espectro's face, ripping the glasses off the bridge of his nose before the bandit could yank his head back.

Suddenly, el Espectro screamed in agony. He released Clint's throat and clamped both hands over his eyes. The albino's unshielded orbs, ultrasensitive to light, had gazed up into the sun.

The Gunsmith's fist crashed into el Espectro's jaw. The bandit fell away from Clint and tried to climb to his feet, one hand still covering his eyes. Clint raised a boot and drove it into the albino's chest.

The kick propelled el Espectro backward. He tumbled awkwardly and fell near the discarded New Line Colt, the back of his head striking the colorful rock. Then the rock moved.

A terrible shriek escaped from el Espectro's lips. He bolted to his feet and tried to claw at the object that clung to his back. Blood oozed from his open mouth as he sunk to his knees and convulsed in a quivering ball.

A large, thickly built reptile still held onto the albino's back, its wart-covered snout pressed against his neck. The "rock" was a beaded lizard which had been sunning itself before el Espectro fell on it.

Clint recalled what Juan Lopez had said about the beaded lizard—that it is more poisonous than a snake and its jaws are like iron. The lizard had bitten el Espectro in the back of the neck, nearly crushing his spinal cord with its powerful teeth and pumping venom directly into the bandit's carotid artery.

The Gunsmith watched el Espectro twitch one last time before the final glimmer of life vanished.

"I guess el Espectro has given up the ghost," Clint commented wearily.

THIRTY-FIVE

Clint rode Duke back to the Black Cathedral, leading the white stallion by its reins with el Espectro's body draped over the saddle. The triumphant *peónes* greeted him with cheers and waved their weapons in victory. Their behavior was a stark contrast to the otherwise grim scene.

Dead bodies—both men and horses—littered the ground. Many were grisly victims of crushing rocks, machetes or multiple gunshots. Yet, the Gunsmith's forces had won. There had been casualties among the *peónes*, but the *bandidos* had been all but wiped out. Only Captain Garcia and two of el Espectro's men had survived the battle.

Both *bandidos* had been injured. One had a crushed foot and a broken wrist. The other had suffered a shattered collarbone and a fractured radius in his right forearm. Garcia's jaw had been broken when Clint kicked him in the face.

The Gunsmith dismounted and the *peónes* swarmed forward to shake his hand and thank him. Clint was relieved to see Marsha Woodland had not been injured. The lovely blonde stood guard over the three prisoners, her Remington held ready, and the expression on her face warned the captives she would welcome a chance to kill any or all of them.

Clint glanced about and saw Father Rameriz approach. The Gunsmith uttered another sigh of relief when he saw the priest had also emerged from the melee unharmed.

"You have returned without injury, my son?" the blind man asked as he took Clint's hand.

"Yes, Father," the Gunsmith assured him. "El Espectro is dead. It's over now."

"Gracias a Dios!" the priest whispered.

"How many people did we lose?" Clint asked grimly.

"Seven have been called to Our Lord," Rameriz answered.

"I'm sorry, Father."

"There was no choice, my son," the priest explained. "Seven died fighting evil. It is better than the alternative, which would have been the death of all my children and a victory for evil, no?"

"That might not be much comfort for the widows and orphans," Clint muttered. "But you're right, Father."

Rameriz hesitated before he said, "A young woman was badly injured. She calls your name."

"Where is she?" Clint asked urgently.

The priest pointed at the base of a rock formation with the bloodstained tip of his cane. Elena Jimenez and an older peasant woman knelt beside a still figure clad in a tattered white dress. Clint hurried forward and stared down at Maria. The front of her dress had been ripped open to apply a bandage to a gunshot wound in her left breast.

"Clint?" she asked hoarsely.

"I'm here, Maria," he replied, kneeling beside her, taking her hand in his. "I'm right here."

"I can not see you very well, my hero," Maria said. "It is dark, no?"

Clint felt the afternoon sun on the back of his neck. "Yeah," he told her. "I guess it is."

"We won, Clint," she smiled.

"We sure did," he agreed, squeezing her hand gently.

"I am glad I will die with friends," Maria commented. "I am glad you are here."

"Maria." Clint felt tears form in his eyes.

"I want you to know," she said softly, "that I love you . . . and . . . if . . ."

Her voice ended with a full gurgle in her throat.

Maria was dead.

THIRTY-SIX

Clint Adams led a small caravan to Fort Juarez. It consisted of Marsha Woodland, Father Rameriz, Elena Jimenez and two *peónes* to help guard their three prisoners—the sole survivors of el Espectro's gang. They also brought the bandit chief's corpse, still slung over the back of his white stallion.

The sentries at the *rurale* post saw their commander riding with a group of peasants. Shouts echoed within the fortress and the gates creaked open. A dozen armed soldiers met the Gunsmith's group, but the *rurales* merely held their rifles and stared at the new arrivals, totally confused. Their *capitán* appeared to be a prisoner of the *peónes* and they had the body of a white-skinned man who appeared to be the fabled el Espectro. How does one handle such a situation?

Their consternation was short lived. Lieutenant Sanchez, the second in command at Fort Juarez, soon joined the *rurales* at the gate. He looked at Garcia and then turned to Clint Adams.

"I think you'd better have a good explanation for this, *señor*," the lieutenant declared.

"You'll find it draped over the back of that white stallion," Clint replied.

"*Cristo!*" Sanchez exclaimed when he recognized

the corpse. "Excuse my language, *padre*." He bowed an apology at Father Rameriz.

"You're looking at Captain Garcia's brother, Rafael," the Gunsmith stated. "Better known as el Espectro. He used to have a reputation as a corpse that rode a white stallion. That story finally became true, although I don't think anyone is afraid of him now."

"You killed him, *señor?*" Sanchez asked.

"The scales of justice got the bite on him, Lieutenant," Clint replied dryly. "Why don't we explain this business in detail? Since you're the new post commander, may I suggest we use your office?"

Captain Garcia was escorted into the office that had formerly belonged to him. Sanchez, Clint Adams, Father Rameriz and Marsha Woodland were also present. The *rurale* lieutenant moved behind the desk. He removed his service revolver from its button-flap holster and placed it on the desk top before he sat behind the big piece of furniture.

Clint told the lieutenant what had occurred in the Devil's Belly over the last three days. Father Rameriz and Marsha supported the Gunsmith's claims. Although Garcia was unable to speak, due to his broken jawbone, he was given a notepad and pencil to allow him to communicate. The *rurale* captain didn't bother to write any denials or even shake his head. He obviously realized such efforts would be useless.

"Your story might be difficult to believe if I hadn't seen the body of el Espectro with my own eyes," Sanchez declared. "Although—I've had some suspicions about Garcia and some of his men for some time."

"I'm sure," Clint said dryly.

"Of course," the lieutenant continued, "you must

BANDIDO BLOOD

understand that he outranked me and I couldn't go to Colonel Morales without proof. Now we can give him plenty of evidence to be certain this disgrace to the uniform of *los rurales* will pay for his terrible crimes."

"That's fine, Lieutenant," the Gunsmith said. "I'll leave the matter in your capable hands. If you don't need us any longer . . ."

"Oh, of course," Sanchez nodded. "You have to take Señorita Woodland back to Texas, no? May I offer to escort you to the city of Magdalena? There is a train station there. You can ride in comfort to the border and easily cross over into Texas at the town called El Paso."

"Thanks, Lieutenant," Clint replied. "Everybody ready to leave?"

"Except you, *capitán*," Sanchez told Garcia as he picked up his revolver and aimed it at the renegade *rurale* officer.

The Gunsmith, Elena, Marsha and Rameriz shuffled out of the office. They'd no sooner stepped into the corridor when they heard a gunshot erupt within the room. Clint reacted instantly and whirled to face the open door of the office, his hand streaking to the modified Colt on his hip.

Lieutenant Sanchez calmly stood over the body of Captain Garcia which lay sprawled on the floor with a bullet hole in his chest. A strand of gray smoke curled from the muzzle of the pistol in Sanchez's hand.

"The prisoner attacked me," the lieutenant said. "I had no choice but to defend myself, no?"

Sanchez would have been more convincing without that smile on his face.

THIRTY-SEVEN

When they emerged from the *rurale* headquarters building, Father Rameriz turned to Clint Adams and placed a hand on his shoulder.

"It is time to say good-bye, my son," he declared. "You must return to your country and we must get back to the village."

"That's a fact." Clint smiled fondly at the priest. "It's been a pleasure getting to know you, Father. You're quite a man."

"*Gracias*." Rameriz nodded. "And I have enjoyed meeting you, although I wish the circumstances could have been different. I hope that some day you will come back when things are not quite so exciting, no? We never did get to finish our chess game."

"No, but we sure checkmated el Espectro. *Vaya con Dios, padre*."

"*Sí*," the priest replied. "Go with God, my son."

Father Rameriz walked across the parade field, his stave probing the ground as he went. The blind man easily located the two male *peónes* who waited with the horses. Elena Jimenez then approached Clint and gazed up at him with her big, beautiful dark eyes.

"I too must return to San José," she said in a choked voice. "My people won a victory today, but they also suffered the loss of seven men. We will have much to do before our village will be the way it was."

"It won't be the way it was, Elena," Clint assured her. "The *bandidos* will never again terrorize or plunder your village."

"That is true," she nodded. "And we have learned we can defend ourselves and that evil triumphs only when one allows it to succeed. Our *padre* told us that you *norteamericanos* believe that freedom is worth fighting for and I know now that this is true. No, San José will not be the same and neither will any of my people. The men have changed because they won a battle against a man they once believed to be an invincible evil spirit. I too have changed because I met you.

"I know you must return to los Estados Unidos," Elena continued. "But one day, you will come back to San José or I will visit your country and find you again, Clint Adams. Somehow, I know we will meet."

The Gunsmith had learned to respect women's intuition—and his own instincts, which told him fate would bring them together again.

"So this is not *adiós*," Elena said, tears escaping from the corners of her eyes. "Just *hasta mañana*, no?"

She kissed him. Her lips were tender, soft and sweet. Clint felt the dampness of her tears on his own cheek as she drew back from his embrace. The girl turned and hurried away to join Father Rameriz and the others.

"Elena!" the Gunsmith called to her.

The girl turned to face him and Clint said, "Until tomorrow, no?"

Elena Jimenez smiled and nodded in reply.

THIRTY-EIGHT

Clint and Marsha Woodland climbed on board the train at Magdalena. Duke hadn't been eager to enter a cattle car. Perhaps the big black gelding recalled a long trip by rail from Brownsville to Yuma when the cattle car had been close to the smoke and soot of the diamond-stack engine.

Clint had patted Duke's neck and assured him that the ride would be brief. The horse wheezed as if to express disgust, but he allowed Clint to lead him into a stall within the car.

"I know, I promised you never again," the Gunsmith told Duke as he scratched the gelding's muzzle. "It won't be all that bad, big fella. We'll be in Texas in less than forty-eight hours. Okay?"

Duke wheezed again, gently—almost a sigh of resignation.

The train left Magdalena half an hour after sundown. Clint felt the big locomotive lurch forward and heard the harsh scream of its whistle and steam hiss from the engine. The Gunsmith wearily carried his saddlebags and Springfield carbine through the corridor to the sleeper car. He hadn't slept in a real bed since he'd left Texas. Maybe a berth on a train didn't qualify, but it was close enough for the Gunsmith.

Clint was glad to be leaving Mexico. His mission into Sonora to rescue Marsha Woodland from el Espectro had been one of the most dangerous and difficult experiences in his life. Clint had lost track of how many dead bodies he'd seen in the last few days. He wasn't even certain how many men he himself had killed.

The price had been high—very high. Juan Lopez and Maria had both virtually died in Clint's arms. The emotional strain and tension had been worse than any physical abuse he'd suffered at the hands of the Ghost's *bandidos*. Those spiritual wounds would need more time to heal than the whip marks on Clint's back. He would never forget Maria's final words—"I love you, Clint . . ."

He found the door to his berth and opened it. Clint's mouth almost fell open when he stared into the sleeper compartment and discovered someone waiting for him. The girl sat on the edge of the bunk, holding a sheet to her torso. Marsha Woodland's long, shapely legs were naked and totally exposed from toe to hip.

"I didn't enter the wrong compartment, did I?" Clint asked lamely.

"You don't want to leave, do you?" Marsha inquired as she removed the sheet to reveal that she wore nothing beneath it.

"Don't ask silly questions, lady," Clint replied.

He quickly shut the door and dumped his belongings in a corner. The girl lay back on the bunk and watched Clint strip off his clothes. She smiled with appreciation at the sight of his naked, leanly muscled physique. The Gunsmith didn't waste any time. He blew out the coal-oil lamp and joined Marsha in bed.

Clint wasn't as tired as he thought. His manhood had

already begun to harden. The Gunsmith slowly ran his hands over Marsha's silken flesh. Her arms snared his neck and pulled him closer. Their lips crushed together, tongues probing eagerly.

"You're probably surprised," Marsha began, purring with pleasure as Clint's mouth moved to her breasts, "to find me here."

"There's no need to explain anything you don't want to, Marsha," he replied. His hands moved to her thighs as his lips continued along the length of her belly, his tongue dragging across her flesh.

"Well, I . . . I . . . told you I'd just need . . . some time," the girl said, her sentence interrupted by gasps in response to Clint's skillful tongue which licked and probed at the blonde triangle between her thighs. "And I decided . . . I've had . . . enough time . . . Ohhh! Clint!"

The Gunsmith mounted her and Marsha quickly steered his stiff erection into her love chamber. Clint entered slowly, gently rocking his member back and forth within Marsha. She clung to him, wrapping her long, strong legs around his hips, locking the ankles together in a firm hold.

Clint thrust harder. She moaned and sobbed with joy and begged for more. The Gunsmith obliged, driving his hungry cock deeper, increasing the speed of each lunge until Marsha bucked and convulsed in a wild orgasm. Clint climaxed as well, pumping his seed into the center of her womanhood.

"Oh, Clint," Marsha sighed. "Can we please do it again?"

"Like I said before, Marsha," the Gunsmith whispered. "Don't ask silly questions."

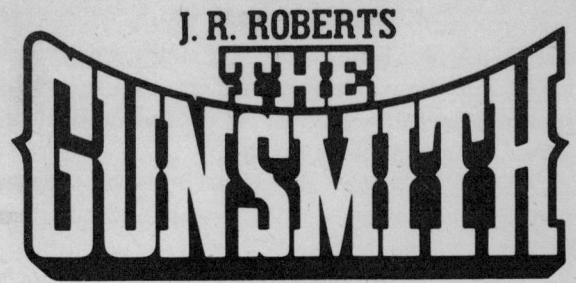

J. R. ROBERTS
THE GUNSMITH
SERIES

☐ 30856-2	THE GUNSMITH #1: MACKLIN'S WOMEN	$2.25
☐ 30857-0	THE GUNSMITH #2: THE CHINESE GUNMEN	$2.25
☐ 30858-9	THE GUNSMITH #3: THE WOMAN HUNT	$2.25
☐ 30859-7	THE GUNSMITH #4: THE GUNS OF ABILENE	$2.25
☐ 30860-0	THE GUNSMITH #5: THREE GUNS FOR GLORY	$2.25
☐ 30861-9	THE GUNSMITH #6: LEADTOWN	$2.25
☐ 30862-7	THE GUNSMITH #7: THE LONGHORN WAR	$2.25
☐ 30863-5	THE GUNSMITH #8: QUANAH'S REVENGE	$2.25
☐ 30864-3	THE GUNSMITH #9: HEAVYWEIGHT GUN	$2.25
☐ 30865-1	THE GUNSMITH #10: NEW ORLEANS FIRE	$2.25
☐ 30866-X	THE GUNSMITH #11: ONE-HANDED GUN	$2.25
☐ 30867-8	THE GUNSMITH #12: THE CANADIAN PAYROLL	$2.25
☐ 30868-6	THE GUNSMITH #13: DRAW TO AN INSIDE DEATH	$2.25
☐ 30869-4	THE GUNSMITH #14: DEAD MAN'S HAND	$2.25
☐ 30872-4	THE GUNSMITH #15: BANDIT GOLD	$2.25
☐ 30886-4	THE GUNSMITH #16: BUCKSKINS AND SIX-GUNS	$2.25
☐ 30887-2	THE GUNSMITH #17: SILVER WAR	$2.25
☐ 30890-2	THE GOLDSMITH #18: HIGH NOON AT LANCASTER	$2.25
☐ 30890-2	THE GOLDSMITH #19: BANDIDO BLOOD	$2.25

Available at your local bookstore or return this form to:

CHARTER BOOKS
Book Mailing Service
P.O. Box 690, Rockville Centre, NY 11571

Please send me the titles checked above. I enclose _____
Include $1.00 for postage and handling if one book is ordered; 50¢ per book for two or more. California, Illinois, New York and Tennessee residents please add sales tax.

NAME _____

ADDRESS _____

CITY _____ STATE/ZIP _____

(allow six weeks for delivery)